The Secret of the
Plant That Ate
Dirty Socks

NANCY McARTHUR lives in Berea, Ohio, a suburb of Cleveland. In addition to writing books, she also teaches journalism part-time at Baldwin-Wallace College and speaks to school groups. *The Secret of the Plant That Ate Dirty Socks* is her fourth book about these characters, and she plans to write more. Her other books for younger readers are *Megan Gets a Dollhouse, Pickled Peppers, The Adventure of the Buried Treasure,* and *The Adventure of the Backyard Sleepout.*

The Secret of the
Plant That Ate
Dirty Socks

Nancy McArthur

AN AVON CAMELOT BOOK

THE SECRET OF THE PLANT THAT ATE DIRTY SOCKS is an original publication of Avon Books. This work has never before appeared in book form.

AVON BOOKS
A division of
The Hearst Corporation
1350 Avenue of the Americas
New York, New York 10019

Copyright © 1993 by Nancy McArthur
Published by arrangement with the author
Library of Congress Catalog Card Number: 92-97474
ISBN: 0-380-76757-0
RL: 5.2

First Avon Camelot Printing: July 1993

CAMELOT TRADEMARK REG. U.S. PAT. OFF. AND IN OTHER COUNTRIES, MARCA REGISTRADA, HECHO EN U.S.A.

Printed in the U.S.A.

OPM   10   9   8   7   6   5   4   3   2   1

In memory of
Richard Allen McArthur

Special thanks to: Susan McArthur, Barbara McArthur, John McArthur, Ellen Krieger, Margy Dwyer, Ericka Luoma, Lynn Luoma, John Luoma, Margaret Stiner, Nick Stiner Riley, Emma Stiner Riley, Mike Spradlin, Jared Earley, Rita Brundage, and Matthew Scruggs and Dina Baldwin of Lorraine Moore's 1990–91 fifth-grade class at Cliffdale Elementary School.

Chapter 1

Michael woke up suddenly when a splash of cold water hit him in the face. He thought his younger brother, Norman, the expert pest, was messing around again with his Super Splasher Water Blaster.

But when he wiped the water from his eyes, he saw that the Blaster was clutched not by Norman, but by Norman's large plant, Fluffy.

Leaping out of bed, Michael slipped on a wet spot on the floor. His own big plant, Stanley, reached out a vine to stop him from falling.

Michael unwound Fluffy's vine from the Blaster.

He snarled at Norman, "How could you turn Fluffy loose with this? If the plants cause any more trouble, we're in even bigger trouble."

Norman replied, "I was just teaching him how to water himself. He's practicing, but his aim isn't very good yet."

Michael yelled, "He got me in the face with that thing!"

"He got me, too," replied Norman. He pointed to a small wet spot on his pajama top.

1

"Good," said Michael. He squeezed the Blaster's trigger and made Norman's wet spot much bigger. Now it covered his entire pajamas and his face.

"I'll get you for this!" yowled Norman.

"No, you won't," retorted Michael. "I just got you for getting me. Now we're even!"

"I didn't get you! Fluffy did!" shouted Norman.

Michael squirted Fluffy. "There!" he exclaimed. "I got Fluffy for both of us. So we're all three even! Now, get out of here!"

"I'm not leaving!" yelled Norman. "Half of this room is mine!" Then he stomped off to the bathroom.

Michael sighed and looked around. Fluffy had also watered the drapes and Stanley as well as the floor.

He heard Mom and Dad's bedroom door open. Mom appeared in the doorway. She saw the wet spots and Michael holding the Water Blaster. She took it away from him.

"I didn't do this," he said. "This is not my fault!"

Just then Norman stomped back in.

"I told you," Mom scolded, "never to make a mess with this thing again!"

"Fluffy did it," explained Norman, "but he didn't mean to!"

Mom exclaimed, "Thank goodness we have to keep these sock-eaters for only six more weeks! Then it'll be good-bye, plants, and we can get back to normal. That is, if we can remember what normal is after all the trouble they've caused."

"Six weeks?" said Norman, looking alarmed.

"Yes," replied Mom. "After school starts the day after tomorrow, then it's only six weeks to Pet Plant Day. I checked the calendar last night."

Norman looked sad. He didn't like to think about giving up Fluffy. Pet Plant Day had seemed so far off.

"Don't worry," Mom told him. "I don't want anything bad to happen to Stanley and Fluffy, even though they drive me crazy. Last night your father and I decided to ask Susan Sparks to find a botanical garden to buy them."

"What's a botanical garden?" asked Norman.

"It's like a zoo, only for plants," explained Mom. "They collect plants from all over the world so people can come and see them."

"Do they put them in cages?" asked Norman.

"Of course not," said Mom. "Some are planted outside, and some are in huge greenhouses."

"No!" shouted Norman, very upset. "You can't put Fluffy and Stanley in a plant zoo!"

"They're beautiful places," said Mom. "And they take wonderful care of plants. Stanley and Fluffy will be happy there."

"No, they won't," said Michael. "Nobody else can care about them as much as we do."

Mom said, "But we all agreed you could keep them only until Pet Plant Day—and only because the principal insisted that we bring them to school for that."

"No fair," whined Norman. "Dr. Sparks lets Max and Sarah keep the plants they grew from Fluffy's seeds at home. Theirs eat socks, too!"

"But theirs," Mom pointed out, "are not almost six feet tall yet. And they don't also drink orange juice and pull themselves around on skateboards. Or escape from the house and have to be chased all over town."

"But Fluffy didn't mean to escape," Norman reminded her.

Michael added, "And they haven't escaped lately."

Mom said, "But they keep getting bigger and hungrier. They're up to four socks a night each. And we never know what they might do next. I know you're very attached to them, but we have to be practical. They're expensive to feed. They keep our lives in an uproar. We can't keep them forever."

Dad wandered in, looking sleepy. "What's happening?" he asked. Noticing the wet spots and the Water Blaster in Mom's hand, he remarked, "Doing a little target practice before breakfast?"

"Very funny," said Mom. "Actually, Fluffy is the one who can't squirt straight. Not me!"

"Amazing!" Dad exclaimed from behind the newspaper at the kitchen table. "It says here scientists found a one-hundred-ten-ton fungus! It covers thirty-seven acres underground in a forest in Michigan."

"How big is that exactly?" asked Michael. He was smearing gobs of strawberry jam on his toast. It slopped over the edges.

Dad replied, "About the size of quite a few football fields put together."

Mom joked, "And we thought *we* had plant problems!"

Norman looked up from his toast, which he was covering neatly with jam. He said huffily, "Fluffy and Stanley are not problems! They're our pets. We love them, and they love us back!"

Michael picked up his toast and went around beside Dad to read the fungus article. "Wow," he said. "They think it's at least one thousand five hundred years old!"

4

"How do they know that?" asked Norman. "Do funguses have birthdays?"

"Of course not!" answered Michael. "It says here they found out it grows eight inches a year. Then they figured it out from that."

Norman remarked, "That must be the biggest plant that ever was in the whole world."

"Nope," said Michael. "A fungus isn't actually a plant. It says so in that book Dr. Sparks sent us." He leaned over the newspaper and took a bite of his toast. A glob of jam oozed over the edge and plopped on the article.

"Watch it! That's right where I'm reading," grumbled Dad. Michael grabbed the nearest paper napkin and wiped up the strawberry goo. They both read on through the big pink spot.

"Aren't you through reading yet?" asked Norman. "Hurry up. I want to see the picture of the giant fungus."

Dad said, "There isn't any picture. The whole thing is underground. There's nothing to see."

Norman looked puzzled. "Then how do the scientists know it's there?" he asked.

"It shoots up honey-colored mushrooms all over the place," said Michael. "But it says here that underground it's 'a dense network of pale, shoestring-sized tentacles that invade and eat dead tree roots,' " he read.

Mom said, "Please don't read things like that out loud while I'm eating."

"Oh, tentacles like an octopus," said Norman. He cut his toast into four equal pieces and stacked them neatly. "This is a toast sandwich," he announced, looking pleased with himself. "I just invented it."

Dad handed the paper over to Michael, who was still reading the article. "This says the tentacles are called rhizomorphs," he continued. "And this species of fungus is called *Armillaria bulbosa*."

"That's a funny name," said Norman.

"It's the scientific name," explained Michael. "Everything has a scientific name."

"Yeah?" said Norman. "What's yours?"

Michael thought a moment. *"Michaelaria smartosa,"* he replied. "And yours would probably be *Normanosa biga pesta*."

"Stop it," said Mom.

Norman waited until she turned away to pass the juice pitcher to Dad. Then he made a horrible face at his brother. When Mom turned back, he was smiling innocently.

He asked, "What're Fluffy's and Stanley's scientific names?"

Dad replied, "That's still a secret. We won't know until Susan Sparks figures out what kind of plants they are."

"When is she going to figure it out?" asked Norman.

Dad said, "Now that you mention it, we haven't heard from her for quite a while. Let's call up the Sparkses and see what's happening."

Since Mom and Susan Sparks had gotten to be good friends, Mom made the call. Sarah Sparks answered the phone.

"My mom's away today at a scientific conference. She'll be back tonight."

Michael listened on the bedroom extension as Mom asked, "How's she doing on identifying our plants?"

"She's been too busy with her regular research, so

she hasn't had a chance to do much on that. But she sent pictures and cuttings to some other botany research places. They didn't know what they were either. They're still checking. It'll be great if they turn out to be a new species. Or even just a rare one.''

Michael asked, ''How are Max's and your plants doing?''

''Fine,'' said Sarah. ''Are yours still eating socks every night?''

''Yes. Why?''

''Ours aren't. Some nights they eat one sock apiece. Then they won't eat any more for one or two nights in a row.''

Michael was astounded. Mom remarked, ''I wish you could tell us how to get Fluffy and Stanley to eat less.''

Michael asked, ''Are you doing anything different with yours?''

''Just paying a lot of attention to them,'' said Sarah. ''Max is still singing to his. Of course, our six plants are together in our greenhouse, so they all have to put up with his little concerts. Wouldn't it be funny if they turned out to eat less because Max sings to them?''

''If his singing is as bad as Norman's,'' Michael suggested, ''maybe it makes them lose their appetite.''

''Actually,'' said Sarah, ''Max is a pretty good singer. Loud, but good.''

After they hung up, Michael wondered whether it might really be possible to get Stanley and Fluffy to eat fewer socks. Or even no socks at all. That would be great. Mom was always complaining about how much the plants' sock suppers cost. If only he could find a way to solve that problem. And if he and Norman could keep the plants from acting up. And if they could get

Mom and Dad to like them. If, if, if. The situation seemed hopeless.

He went into his and Norman's room. Stanley and Fluffy stood motionless, as they usually were during the day. To look at them now, no one would ever guess what weird things they did at night. It was a spectacular sight when they picked up socks with their vines and sucked them into some of their leaves, which were curled up like ice cream cones. They did this with a loud *schlurrrp,* followed by a hearty burp. Then Fluffy made a noise that sounded like "ex" because Norman had tried to teach his plant to say, "Excuse me."

Michael had gotten so used to having Stanley around that he didn't want to think about what life would be like without his tall, leafy friend.

He whispered to Stanley, "I'm not giving up. I'll keep trying to find a way to keep you and Fluffy somehow." Michael sighed. Stanley put a vine around his shoulder.

Chapter 2

The whole family was going shopping to buy things the boys needed for school. But first Mom made Norman try on some of Michael's old clothes that she had been saving until Norman grew into them. She also made Michael try on practically all his things to see what he had outgrown. Then she made a list of what to shop for: for Michael, lots of new clothes; for Norman, just brown pants, shoes, and a couple of shirts.

"No fair," whined Norman. "He always gets all new clothes, and I don't!"

"That's not true," said Mom. "You do get some new things."

Dad pointed out, "You don't have to wear Michael's hand-me-down socks anymore. He doesn't have any left to hand down. Stanley eats them all as soon as they're dirty."

"Right," said Michael. "And I have to change socks every afternoon so there'll be four dirty ones a night for him. You've got it easy 'cause Fluffy only eats clean ones."

9

Norman said glumly, "I wish Stanley ate your other clothes, too."

"Cheer up," said Mom. She pulled a blue and green ski jacket from a storage box. "Remember? The year before last you used to say you wished you had a jacket just like Michael's. Now it's yours."

Norman had forgotten about that jacket. He put it on, looked in the mirror, and stood there smiling at himself.

The night before school started, Norman fell asleep right away, but Michael lay awake for a long time. He wondered what his new teacher would be like. Who would be in his class? How hard would math be this year? And how could he keep the plants from being sent away forever?

Stanley lifted a vine from Michael's pillow and touched his hand. Michael fell asleep.

Norman got up early as usual. He bustled around the room, singing and slamming drawers. Michael snuggled down, determined to stay in bed as long as possible.

Then Michael heard a strange new noise, *Swoosh, swoosh, swoosh, swoosh.* What weird new activity were the plants up to now? He peeked out from under his blanket. The plants were doing nothing, but Norman was wearing his new brown corduroy pants. With every step, his pants legs rubbed together. *Swoosh, swoosh, swoosh, swoosh.*

"Shut up your pants!" snarled Michael.

Norman hadn't been happy to find his new pants were so noisy. But he was delighted to discover that he had a new way to drive his brother crazy. He walked around and around the room, *swoosh*ing like mad.

"Stop it!" yelled Michael.

Norman kept *swoosh*ing.

Michael gritted his teeth. Obviously the more he objected, the more Norman would do it.

He got out of bed and said casually, "Come to think of it, your noisy pants are a good thing. You won't be able to sneak up on me. I'll hear you coming a mile away!"

Norman tried to think of a smart comeback. He had never thought much about sneaking up on his brother, but he liked the idea. He smiled.

"I can, too, sneak up on you," he boasted. "See?" He started walking bowlegged with his knees bent so his pants didn't rub together. Sure enough, this was perfect for silently sneaking up.

Mom looked into their room and asked Norman, "What on earth are you doing? A chimpanzee imitation?"

He replied, "I'm making my pants be quiet so I can sneak up."

Mom said, "Then sneak on out to the kitchen and surprise your father. Michael, get a move on and get dressed."

At school the principal, Mr. Leedy, was at the front door to greet everyone.

The halls were noisy with kids chattering excitedly on the way to their rooms. Michael found the right door and hurried to get a desk by the window. He hoped Mrs. Black would let them sit wherever they wanted. Jason Greensmith and Chad Palmer came in and took window seats, too. Kimberly Offenberg and Pat Jenkins took seats by the door, and other girls sat near them.

Mrs. Black began checking off the names on her list.

11

Mr. Leedy stopped in to tell them they were going to have a great year. A tinny squawk from the metal box on the wall signaled morning announcements on the public address system. Students took turns announcing events, achievements, and birthdays, and reading aloud or singing. Most of them liked doing this because it seemed like being on the radio.

Today a boy led the pledge of allegiance, and a trio of girls sang the school song in wavery voices.

A boy and girl Michael had never seen before turned out to have moved to town over the summer. Since they had never heard of Pet Plant Day, Mrs. Black explained about it. She assured them they had six weeks to grow or get a plant to bring. To prepare for the big day, she announced, they were going to do a plant unit with reading, writing, science, history, social studies, and math.

"As part of this," she added, "you are going to do a research report about your kind of plant and identify it by its scientific botanical name."

Michael wondered what to do about that. How do you report on your kind of plant when you don't know what kind it is? He hoped Dr. Sparks would hurry up.

During recess, Jason asked Michael, "Do you want a good deal on some video games?" He reeled off the names of about ten.

Jason was good at making trades and deals. He also sometimes left out a few facts. Earlier he had helped himself to some of Stanley's seeds and sold them to lots of other kids while Michael was away on vacation. Tracking down and buying back all the baby plants that had started growing had been a big mess. Jason had helped Michael do it, and things had turned out OK because the family had taken the baby plants to Dr. Sparks for research.

Although a good deal on video games sounded tempting, Michael knew better now than to jump at one of Jason's deals. He wondered if there was something wrong with the games.

"Where did you get them?" he asked.

"They're mine," said Jason.

"Why are you selling them?"

"I played them enough. I want the money to use for other things."

"I'll think about it," said Michael.

"Let me know soon," said Jason. "I'm giving you first chance before I talk to anyone else. How are your plants doing?"

"Fine."

Jason asked, "Have they done anything else weird lately besides eat socks and OJ?"

Michael didn't want to let Jason in on all the details. He answered, "They've learned to do a few other little things."

"Like what?"

"Promise not to tell?"

"Of course. I've known about the sock-eating ever since the sleep-over at your house, and I haven't told anyone. Your father made me promise not to."

"Well, Norman taught Fluffy how to play ball."

Jason chuckled. "That's great. Anything else?"

"Both plants grab on to furniture sometimes with their vines and pull themselves around on their skateboards."

"Cool," said Jason. Then he asked, "Do they ever slap your hands? Or grab your arm and squeeze so hard, it hurts?"

"Of course not! They would never do that. They love us. Fluffy even hugs Norman. He never squashes him. What made you think of things like that?"

"Just wondering," Jason replied. "Are they still burping?"

Michael laughed. "Yeah, louder than ever!"

That afternoon in class, Michael had trouble paying attention to what Mrs. Black was teaching. Six more weeks, he kept thinking. Then the plants would be gone. And why were Sarah and Max's plants not eating socks every night? There must be a logical explanation. But what? Could they be eating something else instead?

"The way plants make their own food," Mrs. Black was saying, "is called photosynthesis." Michael started paying attention. "A plant uses four ingredients to make food inside itself," she explained. She wrote on the board: "Chlorophyll—green coloring in plant cells. Water. Light. Carbon dioxide."

Michael had read about this before but had not given it much thought. He knew that people breathed in oxygen and breathed out carbon dioxide and that plants did the opposite.

"Plants absorb carbon dioxide from the air," Mrs. Black went on. "Then they give off oxygen. Some people think that plants grow better if you talk to them." She smiled. "But when you talk to plants, you're breathing more carbon dioxide at them. Maybe that's why they like being talked to."

Everybody laughed except Michael. Norman was always blabbing or singing to Fluffy. So his plant was getting extra carbon dioxide. Could that be giving him a bigger appetite? Max was singing to their plants, too. All the plants had the same amount of chlorophyll. When they had visited the Sparkses, Sarah and Max were watering their plants as much as Michael and Norman did.

Michael looked back at the board. That left one thing. Light. Of course! Max and Sarah's plants lived in their home greenhouse with glass walls and roof. They had sunlight all day long. Stanley and Fluffy lived by the window in Michael and Norman's room. The sun came in only for a little while in the morning.

Michael decided to experiment. Would more light help Stanley and Fluffy make more food inside and cut down their big appetite for socks?

Chapter 3

When Michael got home from school, he found Norman in the kitchen making a baked bean sandwich. Michael was hungry, so he made one, too. Norman put a plate under his sandwich to catch the beans that fell out as he ate it. Michael walked around as he ate his, leaving a trail of lost beans all over the room. He started explaining his experiment idea to Norman. But he should never have tried to explain photosynthesis to him.

Telling Norman that he breathed out carbon dioxide sent him running to Mom to complain that Michael said he had bad breath.

Mom told Michael, "Don't say mean things to him!"

"I didn't," protested Michael. "Carbon dioxide is not bad breath. It's good breath to plants."

Norman didn't believe him. He just sat at the kitchen table and glared.

Michael announced, "I've got good news. There might be a way to cut down on the amount of socks the plants eat."

"That would be good," said Mom. "It'd save us some money over the next six weeks."

He explained.

Norman forgot about being mad at Michael. "Yay! Let's do it!" he said.

Mom said, "It makes sense. Sort of. I guess it would be worth a try. Maybe the living room window would be best. It's on the north side of the house, so there's more light there."

"You don't understand," Michael said. "We need more light than that to see if this will work. We have to put the plants outside from early morning till the sun goes down. That'll be as much light as they'd get in a greenhouse like the Sparkses'. And it won't cost anything."

"You want to leave them out there all day while you're at school? Absolutely not. They might escape again."

"But this would be a great scientific breakthrough," said Michael. "Dr. Sparks lets Sarah and Max do experiments."

"Just put them out after school while you can watch them," Mom suggested.

"But that's not enough. We need all day to see if it will work!"

"Start with after school," Mom decided. "See how that works for a few days. Then Saturday and Sunday they can be out all day."

The boys rolled the plants out into the backyard for the rest of the afternoon.

With Stanley and Fluffy parked side by side in the middle of the grass, there was nothing within reach of their vines that they could grab on to. They couldn't pull themselves anywhere. Michael pointed this out to Mom.

"Watch them anyway," she insisted. They took half-hour turns plant-sitting. Norman's friend Bob came over and they kicked a soccer ball around. Then Michael came out with a plant book to read.

When Dad came home from work, Norman got to him first.

"We're doing an experiment," he said excitedly. "If our plants stay out in the sunshine all day, they might not eat as many socks!"

Dad asked, "Where on earth did you get this far-fetched idea?"

"Michael thought it up," replied Norman, getting himself off the hook in case the plan didn't work.

Outside, a little brown sparrow fluttered to a landing on Stanley, who didn't seem to mind. Michael, deep into reading his book, didn't even notice.

Dad came out and listened to Michael's plan. "We'll see," he said.

"Dinner's almost ready," called Mom from the back door. "Michael, your turn to set the table."

When they came in, Mom said, "Better get the plants in now."

"They'll be OK out there awhile longer," said Dad. "They're not going anywhere."

Outside, the brown sparrow returned to perch on Fluffy. An orange cat approached sneakily, perhaps attracted by the bird. The bird flew away, but the cat came closer. It sniffed at Fluffy's skateboard, pot, and lower leaves. Then it chomped a leaf and began chewing it.

Fluffy whipped a vine around the cat's middle, lifted it a couple of feet in the air, and dropped it. The startled cat spit out the leaf and streaked away.

*　　　*　　　*

They brought the plants in after dinner. That night the boys put out the regular four socks for each. In the morning, they were all gone as usual.

Michael decided not to buy any video games from Jason, although he had saved a lot of money from mowing lawns. He had been fantasizing about someday saving enough to buy a home greenhouse for Stanley and Fluffy.

Now this seemed impossible, but he decided to hang on to all his money anyway, just in case. Right now there was nothing he wanted except to keep Stanley, and money wouldn't buy that.

After some afternoons of sitting in the sun, the plants looked particularly good, but they were still eating heartily.

Saturday morning, Norman took Fluffy out as soon as the sun came up. By the time Michael got up two hours later, Norman had nagged him every fifteen minutes or so to get up and take Stanley out. It was a warm, sunny day. It seemed like summer except for the few crisp leaves fallen on the grass.

After breakfast Mom took Michael along to the Save-A-Lot discount store to buy socks. On the way in, they ran into Jason. He was on his way out, carrying a big bag.

"Hi," said Michael. "What did you buy?"

"Just some little stuff," said Jason.

Michael shrugged. "See you around," he said.

"Yeah, see you," replied Jason. Michael saw him ride away on his bike, holding the bag with one arm. It didn't look heavy.

He caught up with Mom in the socks aisle. "They're sold out of fudge ripple," she said, pointing to the empty space where the white socks with brown stripes usually sat. She started selecting brown and pink ones. "The plants'll have to be satisfied with chocolate and strawberry," she said.

"Stanley won't mind," he said, "but Fluffy's not going to be happy. Fudge ripple's his favorite." He picked up some white ones. "We need vanilla, too," he said.

On the way to the checkout counter, he saw a deluxe pocketknife with lots of attachments, and decided to buy it for himself. He had always wanted one of those. Mom said OK, as long as he promised never to open it up. Michael was pleased with his purchase. Now if he decided to whittle a stick or open a can away from home, he was all set.

Back home, Norman and Dad were supposed to be watching the plants. But Dad was busy puttering in the garage. He thought Norman was watching. Norman thought Dad was watching. He wandered down the street with Bob and stopped to talk to Mrs. Smith, his favorite neighbor.

So they didn't see the little dog that trotted into the backyard. It sniffed the plants thoroughly. Then it yapped at them as if telling them to get out of their own yard.

Stanley grabbed the dog and wrapped one vine around its snout to shut it up for a moment. Then he let the dog go. It galloped away.

A little later a squirrel came by and started digging

in Fluffy's pot to bury an acorn. Fluffy snatched up the squirrel and dropped it. It ran up the nearest tree and clung upside down to the trunk, chattering angrily.

That afternoon Dad cleaned some junk out of the garage, and Mom cleaned out the refrigerator. Since Dad had already filled up the two trash cans by the garage, she put the discards from the refrigerator in a plastic bag beside the cans.

Dad warned her that the stuff in the bag might attract a cat or raccoon. She replied, "If they'd like to eat old, moldy leftovers, they're welcome to them."

At bedtime Michael and Norman put out the socks, with high hopes.

"This is the first whole day of sun they've had," said Michael. "Maybe we'll know in the morning if it's working."

As they were going to sleep, Norman asked, "If we can get them to stop eating socks, do you think Mom and Dad will let us keep them?"

"I don't know if that'll be enough to make them change their minds. But we have to keep trying. If this doesn't work, we'll try something else."

"Like what?"

"I don't know. I wish we could find a way to make Mom and Dad like the plants as much as we do. Then they couldn't get rid of them."

Norman said, "Maybe we could teach Fluffy and Stanley to help around the house. Run the vacuum. Make the beds. Do the laundry."

Michael chuckled. "I'd hate to turn them loose with

a vacuum cleaner. Maybe they could dust.'' This struck him as so funny that he began to laugh. Norman joined in the giggling.

When they finally calmed down, Michael said, ''Maybe in the morning there'll be some socks left.''

Norman was so excited about this possibility that he woke up so early, it was still dark out. He turned on the lamp between the beds.

There, on the floor, were two socks, one beside each plant!

''Yay!'' yelled Norman. He shook Michael awake and showed him. Michael was thrilled. The experiment was starting to work! He got up and put the two socks away so Stanley and Fluffy couldn't change their minds. Then he went back to sleep.

Norman looked out the window. The sky was just beginning to get a little lighter. He passed some time rolling a ball across the floor to Fluffy, who knocked it back to him.

As soon as the sky grew pale blue, Norman put on his robe and slippers and rolled Fluffy outside.

Fluffy stretched a little, rustling his leaves. Near the trash cans a small animal had ripped a hole in the plastic bag and was rummaging in the garbage. While Norman was there, it ducked down and stayed very still. After he went back in the house, the animal poked its head up to look at Fluffy.

This time it wasn't a yappy little dog. It wasn't a cat, or a squirrel, or even a raccoon. Its glossy black fur was striped with white.

The skunk approached cautiously, sniffing as it came closer. Fluffy's leaves bristled. The skunk came too close. The plant didn't wait to get pawed or clawed. He whipped out a couple of vines and grabbed the little animal to lift it and move it away. But the frightened skunk raised its tail and sprayed all over Fluffy. The plant was so startled that he let go. The skunk ran away.

The smell was truly horrible. Slowly it drifted on the breeze.

Chapter 4

A little later, Dad, who was sleeping on the side of the bed near the open window, got a whiff and woke up. He nudged Mom and said, "There's a skunk smell coming in the window!"

Mom mumbled sleepily, "Then close the window."

He got out of bed and closed it. "I hope it's not in our yard," he said. "I'm going to check."

Mom mumbled, "It probably just had a run-in with a dog and took off."

As Dad passed the door of the boys' room, Norman bounded out to see what was happening. When Dad told him there was a skunk in the neighborhood, Norman followed him.

"I never smelled a skunk before," he said eagerly.

"After you've smelled one," Dad assured him, "you'll never want to smell another one."

Norman said, "I have to bring Fluffy back in. He won't like a bad smell like that."

Dad asked, "You think Fluffy can smell things?"

"Sure," said Norman. "Don't you think so?"

"I guess it wouldn't surprise me," said Dad. He opened the back door.

"Pee-yew!" exclaimed Norman.

They went out toward Fluffy. The smell got unbearably stronger. Dad said, "Hold your nose and breathe through your mouth. Or better yet, don't breathe at all." As Norman reached for Fluffy with his non-nose-holding hand, Dad grabbed his wrist.

"Don't touch," he warned. His voice sounded silly because he was holding his nose. "The smell is coming from Fluffy! Don't get it on you!"

Fluffy looked stunned. His leaves drooped. His vines slumped, dragging on the ground.

"He's passed out!" cried Norman as loudly as he could with his nose squashed shut.

"Back in the house!" instructed Dad. "We need some tomato juice!"

"No!" said Norman. "We can't eat breakfast now! We have to save Fluffy!"

Dad let go of his own nose and dragged Norman into the house. Then he explained, "The tomato juice isn't for us. It's what you use to kill the smell."

"How does that work?" asked Norman.

"I don't know," said Dad, "but that's the age-old remedy."

"But Fluffy only eats orange juice. He's never had tomato juice. And he can't eat it when he's passed out!"

Dad looked in the refrigerator and then started searching cupboards. He said patiently, "The tomato juice is to wash the smell off. If a dog gets sprayed by a skunk, you give the dog a bath in tomato juice."

Norman looked at him suspiciously. "Are you sure?"

"I'm positive," said Dad.

Norman said, "I don't see how Fluffy is going to lie his whole self down in the bathtub. He's too tall."

25

"This isn't something you do indoors," replied Dad. "I can't find any tomato juice. Go wake up your mother."

Norman loved to wake people up. He got Michael up, too. When they assembled in the kitchen, Mom yawned and said, "You don't need me for this. You guys go ahead and take care of it."

Dad replied, "We need you to figure out how much tomato juice to buy. I don't want to make two trips if I guess wrong. And what stores are open this early?"

Mom looked out the window, trying to picture how much juice it would take to cover Fluffy. She estimated about six quarts. "If that's too much," she said, "we can always drink the leftovers. But how are you going to pour it all over the plant without missing any spots? And what about the mess all over the grass?"

Michael said, "Tomato juice has salt in it. Salt can kill plants." Norman looked alarmed.

"We'll pour it on and rinse it off so fast, it won't have a chance to hurt Fluffy," said Dad.

"But what about the grass?" said Mom. "And rinsing the juice off with the hose is going to get it all over. You better do it on the driveway."

Dad protested, "Then we might have red stains on the concrete."

Michael added, "After we hose it, there'll be red water running down the drive, across the sidewalk, into the street. It'll look like we murdered something in the driveway."

Mom said, "The longer we sit here doing nothing, the longer Fluffy will be smelling up the neighborhood."

"And he's passed out," wailed Norman. "The smell's going to kill him!"

26

Michael joked, "We should take him to a car wash. That way we could rinse the whole mess down a drain."

"Good idea," said Dad. "But how do we get him there?"

Norman said, "Michael could tow him with his bike, the way he did Stanley on the Fourth of July."

Now Michael was sorry he had brought this up. "But Fluffy doesn't know how to hang on the way Stanley does," he said. "Besides, he's passed out."

Dad said, "We've got some rope in the garage. So he won't have to hang on. We can go to that do-it-yourself car wash. It's coin-operated. There aren't any attendants to tell us we can't wash a plant that smells bad."

Norman said, "I can put the juice in my Blaster and squirt it all over Fluffy. That'll be really fast."

"OK," said Mom, "but let's take a pail and sponges in case that doesn't work. We can buy tomato juice on the way at that twenty-four-hour convenience store up on Beech Street." She got out some plastic gloves.

"These are for whoever's going to touch Fluffy to tie the rope, and it isn't going to be me."

Dad took the gloves and rope, and Norman came with him. He held Dad's nose for him, because Dad needed both hands to tie the rope around the base of Fluffy's main stalk. Soon they were ready to roll.

Michael led the way on his bike. Fluffy, with his vines tucked around him so they didn't drag, rolled behind him. Mom, Dad, and Norman followed slowly in the car with the windows closed. Mom was driving so Dad could get out to help fast if Michael had a problem.

Norman kept yelling, "Hurry up! That smell's gonna kill him!"

Fortunately, few people were out this early. The strange little parade passed almost unnoticed. They made a quick stop at the store. Dad had rushed off without his wallet, so Mom ran in to buy the juice.

At the car wash, all six stalls were empty. Michael towed Fluffy into the one farthest from the street. Each stall, with a roof and two side walls, was open at both ends. Fluffy looked somewhat revived from the fresh air, but he was still in pretty bad shape.

They had forgotten to bring a can opener, so Michael opened the cans with his new pocket knife. Dad poured tomato juice into the pail, and Norman filled his Blaster. They applied juice to Fluffy with the Blaster and sponges, each using one hand while he held his nose with the other. The smell began to fade.

Mom got out of the car, which she had parked by the vacuum machine just outside the stall. She put some quarters in. The powerful vacuum roared and began sucking her shirttail in. She wrestled it away and put the huge vacuum tube inside the car to suck up crumbs and other assorted little nuggets of crud that a family car collects.

Dad was reading the complicated directions on one wall that explained how to operate the wash equipment. There was a big circle on the wall with different choices and a dial in the middle to select.

A long black hose looped down from the ceiling. It hung from a large spring that made moving it easy and kept it from tangling. The long metal spout end of the hose was stuck in a holder by the wall.

On the opposite wall hung another hose with a big brush on the end. The sign next to it said FOAMING BRUSH. READ DIRECTIONS BEFORE USING.

Dad turned the dial. He bypassed Tire Cleaner, Cleaning Solution, Foam, and Lemon Spray Wax. He went directly to Rinse.

When the boys finished deluging Fluffy with tomato juice, Dad took the hose from the holder.

"Let me do it," said Michael.

"No, me," whined Norman. "It's my plant!" They both grabbed at the hose.

"Take turns," Dad decided. He handed the hose to Norman.

"Ready?" asked Dad.

"Ready," said Norman. Dad plunked some quarters into the machine by the dial. Glowing red numbers began counting down the seconds of the two minutes before the money ran out.

With a loud whoosh, the hose came alive in Norman's hands. Water spurted so powerfully that it whipped around like a snake trying to escape. The first blast splashed Michael.

"Aim at Fluffy!" yelled Michael. "Not me!"

Dad helped Norman control the hose. The force of the spray would have been fine for a car, but it almost knocked Fluffy over. Dad and Norman backed off. Now the spray hit Fluffy like a big rainstorm. The tomato juice ran off into the drain.

"This is better than my Blaster!" yelled Norman gleefully. Soon the red numbers ticked off: 5, 4, 3, 2, 1, 0. The hose stopped with a clunk.

Michael grumbled, "Why does he always get ME all wet?"

"He didn't mean to," Dad said. "Look on the bright side. It could have been worse. You could have been Lemon Spray Waxed."

Michael didn't find this funny. He eyed the hose and the dial. He thought about turning it to Lemon Spray Wax and going after Norman. Or Foam would be even better. But he didn't have any quarters.

Norman rolled Fluffy out of the stall into the sunshine. His wet leaves had perked up and looked almost back to normal. Norman gave the plant a hug and got himself all wet, so Michael gave up on his imaginary plot for revenge.

Mom said, "As long as we're here, we might as well do the car." Dad agreed. Mom drove it into the stall. Michael didn't want to take a chance on getting any wetter. He opened the passenger door and got in.

Dad turned the dial to Cleaning Solution and started putting quarters in. Moving fast and keeping an eye on the timer, he sprayed the whole car.

As Michael relaxed, watching the liquid flood down the windows, it occurred to him that this Fluffy-skunk mess was one more reason his parents would use to get rid of the plants. He wondered what else he and Norman could do. Then he recalled Norman's nutsy house chore idea from last night. Maybe it wasn't such a silly idea after all.

Dad put more quarters in. He turned the dial to Foam and went around the car to get the foaming brush on the wall. But Norman was too fast for him. He had grabbed the brush and started smearing the car with it. He looked so happy that Dad let him keep going.

"Don't go too fast with that thing," cautioned Dad. "You're missing some spots."

"But the timer," said Norman.

"Don't worry," said Dad. "We'll put more quarters in. I'll have to do the high parts you can't reach."

Michael saw through the windshield that Norman missed a big spot on the hood. He couldn't resist needling his brother about this. He opened his window and was about to open his mouth when the foaming brush came by, with Norman on the other end of it. It foamed him right in the face.

"Oops," said Norman, moving the brush on down the car door. "You shouldn't have opened the window."

Michael wiped the foam off his face with the bottom of his shirt and yelled at Norman. Mom hit the power button on the control panel on her side and shut his window. Michael was still yelling, but Norman could hardly hear him.

Norman foamed the window, erasing Michael from view. Dad took the brush from him.

Mom told Michael to calm down.

Michael complained, "He gets away with everything!"

"Not everything," Mom pointed out. "And you get away with your share, too."

Dad was almost finished when the timer flashed zero and the foam cut off. He rapped on the driver's-side window.

"Give me some more quarters," he said. Mom searched her handbag.

"I don't have any more," she replied. "I used some on the vacuum."

Dad said, "There must be a change machine around this place somewhere."

Mom said, "I don't have any money left to change. I spent the rest of my cash on tomato juice."

The foam was drying on the car. "We'll go home and rinse it off with the hose," Dad decided. They got Fluffy lined up for towing. Michael, still grumbling, pedaled away with the plant. Mom used the windshield wipers to smear a big hole in the foam to see to drive.

At home they found Bob waiting for Norman and bouncing a soccer ball off their garage door.

"You took Fluffy for a ride?" he asked. "Where did you go so early?"

Norman explained, "Fluffy got stunk up by a skunk. We had to take him to the car wash and blast him with tomato juice to get off the skunk gunk."

"Cool," said Bob. "What happened to your car? Is that skunk gunk?"

"No, it's car wash foam. I got to smear it all over."

"Lucky you," said Bob wistfully. "You always get to do great stuff!"

As Mom went into the house, she was talking to herself. They all heard her say, "Thank goodness, only five more weeks!"

Michael decided to start house chore training right away.

Chapter 5

After breakfast, Norman went over to Bob's to make a sign on their computer. BEWARE OF PLANT, it said. KEEP YOUR HANDS AND PAWS OFF THIS PLANT! OR ELSE!! THIS MEANS YOU!!!! For good measure, they added a skull and crossbones at the bottom.

Mom said, "It looks very nice." She promised she would take him to get the sign laminated one day next week.

Michael asked, "Do you really think an animal is going to read that?" Norman ignored him.

Dad said, "You certainly are a good sign writer." Norman beamed with pride.

Late that morning, Dr. Sparks called, sounding excited.

"I have amazing news," she told Mom.

"What happened?" asked Mom. She motioned to Michael to go pick up the other phone.

"I'm calling from a motel," Dr. Sparks said. "I'm attending a scientific society luncheon here. When I walked into the lobby, there was a plant just like yours

33

sitting on the front desk. So it might not be a rare or unknown species after all.''

"But where did it come from?'' asked Mom.

"A maid found it when she cleaned a room, but she forgot which room she found it in. They put it in the lost-and-found box, thinking the owner would call. But nobody did. They put it on the desk, where it would get some light. It's been growing there ever since. The woman at the desk said it looks so weird that everybody likes it.''

"Are they missing any socks?'' asked Michael.

"No, when I asked about that, she looked at me strangely. She said a few gloves have disappeared from the lost-and-found box. But the desk is open all night, and the lights are on around the clock. So this plant doesn't know when it's night.

"Anyway,'' she continued, "they're looking up the names and addresses from the weekend the plant was found. When I track down whoever lost it, we'll find out where they got it. That may help us identify it.''

"Where is this motel?'' asked Mom.

"Just off Interstate 271, about an hour from my house.''

"Could that by any chance be the Hampton Inn?'' asked Mom.

"Why, yes,'' said Dr. Sparks. "Do you know it?''

Mom turned back the pages of the wall calendar by the phone that she used to keep track of the family's activities.

"Was the plant found the weekend of April twentieth?''

"Yes,'' said Dr. Sparks. "Oh. Wasn't that when you

34

and the boys came to visit us and brought a carload of little plants?''

"Right," said Mom. "We stayed there and took the plants into our room for the night. Do you remember how many we delivered to you?''

"Twenty-six," replied Dr. Sparks.

Michael said, "We left home with twenty-seven."

"Mystery solved," said Mom.

"Rats," said Dr. Sparks. "I thought this one in the lobby was the big clue to where the plants came from. I guess I've been reading too many mystery stories. As a scientist, I should know better than to jump to conclusions.''

Dr. Sparks put the desk manager on the phone. Mom explained how they had lost the plant and asked her to give it to Dr. Sparks.

When Dr. Sparks got back on the phone, Michael asked, "Do you have any idea when you might find out what kind of plants these are? I have to make a report in school pretty soon."

"Not yet," she replied. "I've been too busy to follow up on it, but I sent inquiries to other botanists who are experts at identifying rare plants. Be patient. Science moves slowly.''

"But I don't know what to do about my report," said Michael.

Dr. Sparks replied, "You can say that they're sub-tropical. I'm sure of that.''

"What's that?''

"They're from a climate that's warm year-round. If you left them outside in the winter, they wouldn't survive.''

Michael said, "I'm doing an experiment with them outside."

"That's great, but don't do it when the weather gets colder," she said. "I want to hear all about it, but I'm late for my meeting. Be sure to keep detailed notes on your experiment. We'll talk soon. 'Bye."

Michael took Norman aside for a conference.

"We have to put our house-chores idea into action right away. We should be able to train the plants to do stuff like that in five weeks if we start now."

"What do you mean 'our idea'?" said Norman. "It was *my* idea!"

"It doesn't matter whose idea it was," said Michael. "The important thing is keeping the plants. I really think if they help around the house, that would get Mom and Dad to like them. Pretty soon it'll be too cold for them to go outdoors, so we can't count on just the more-sunshine experiment. We need something else. Fluffy's skunk crisis sure didn't help any."

"It wasn't Fluffy's fault!" said Norman indignantly.

"I know," said Michael. "I'm just glad he's OK. But we also have to keep both plants out of trouble while we're working on these other things."

"OK," said Norman. "Let's start training in the morning. You'll have to get up a lot earlier. Before Mom and Dad get up is the only time we can teach the plants without them knowing what we're doing."

Michael hated getting up early. But for Stanley he was willing to do it. He added, "We can teach them on Wednesdays after school, too. Mom doesn't get home from her part-time job until five-thirty or six on Wednesdays."

When they were getting ready for bed that night, Michael remarked, "I'm tired of waiting for Dr. Sparks to find out whether Stanley and Fluffy are an endangered species or one that's never been discovered before. I want to know where they came from."

"They came in the mail," Norman reminded him, "when they were just beans."

"They came from some offer I sent for," said Michael, "but I never could remember which offer it was. I wish I hadn't lost the leaflet that came in the package."

Norman suggested, "Maybe it's somewhere in all that junk of yours in the closet."

"No, I looked through that stuff a long time ago."

Norman said, "We just have to wait for Dr. Sparks to figure out Stanley and Fluffy's secret identity."

"Well, I'm going to keep looking in books," said Michael. "Since they eat socks and act up at night, maybe they're related to plants that eat bugs or ones whose flowers only open at night."

"That's weird," said Norman, climbing into his bed.

"Not any weirder than Stanley and Fluffy," said Michael.

Mom came in to bring clean clothes and say good night. Michael draped one of Stanley's vines over her shoulder.

"See?" he said. "Stanley likes you."

"That's nice," said Mom.

He tried to think up some more positive things to say.

"Stanley and Fluffy do a good job of cleaning the air for us. They take in the carbon dioxide we breathe and give off oxygen."

Mom remarked, "Any plants can do that. After they're gone, we can get some little ones that don't do anything except that."

"But big plants are better than little ones."

"I don't think so," said Mom.

Norman added, "They are, too!"

Michael tried to think of something else good about big plants. "Big ones make shade," he said. "Little ones can't do that."

"We don't need shade in the house," said Mom.

Michael tried again. "They're hard to see around," he said. "They can be a room divider."

"Yeah," said Norman helpfully. "What room would you like them to divide?"

"We don't need any rooms divided," said Mom.

Michael said, "For Halloween we can throw sheets over them to be spooky ghost decorations."

"That way," added Norman, "they'd also scare off burglars, in case we ever get any burglars. And for Thanksgiving we can make them Pilgrim costumes. They'll look great!"

"You're very creative thinkers," said Mom, giving them each a hug, "but the plants will be spending those holidays someplace else."

Chapter 6

Early the next morning the boys started teaching the plants how to dust. Norman also decided to teach Fluffy how to water the plants in the backyard with the Water Blaster, to save Dad some yard work. Michael hoped to train Stanley to lift things up to the top shelves in kitchen cupboards. He thought Mom would appreciate not having to get the stepladder to reach high places.

At school, Norman's class was working on collecting seeds and matching them up with what grows from them. Michael's class was identifying trees. A member of the local historical society visited his class and showed slides of the oldest trees in town. She also told them what was happening in history when those trees were planted. The oldest one she told them about was a two-hundred-year-old oak in the park.

Mr. Jones, the custodian, was organizing the display areas to be set up in the gym for Pet Plant Day. The students had to sign up in advance, telling whether they were bringing short plants or tall ones, so he would have enough of the right kinds of platforms and shelves ready.

Some art classes had made brown crepe paper vines and stuck them with tape all over the hall walls. Students received green paper leaves to write the titles of their favorite books on. The vines were filling up fast.

Mrs. Black made a reading tree for her room with a big dead branch she found. She stuck it upright in a pail of gravel so it wouldn't keel over. The kids got to hang a leaf on it for every book they read on their own.

The school parents' association was making plans to get a seedling from a historic tree to plant in front of the building. Mom volunteered for this. The committee was coming over to their house on Saturday.

It poured rain that morning, so the boys kept the plants inside. Norman went with Dad to do errands. Michael stayed home to go through some plant books from the library to see if he could find any clues to what kind Stanley and Fluffy might be.

When he looked out the window to see if the rain had stopped, he spotted Mrs. Kramer coming along the sidewalk with her little boy, Kyle.

The toddler kept pulling his hand out of hers and trying to dash away. She grabbed him as he darted toward the street. At the edge of the yard next door, he scampered through some defenseless petunias and stomped them flat.

Mrs. Kramer scooped him up and carried him, wiggling and squawking, up the front walk. Apparently he wanted to go back and finish off the rest of the petunias.

Mom answered the door. "Oh," she said unenthusiastically. "You brought Kyle. Isn't he cute."

40

"Yes," said Mrs. Kramer, "Mary and Ashley had twirling lessons this morning, and my husband had to work. So I had to bring Kyle." She smiled proudly as she clutched her squirming son. "He's such a little terror." She put him down.

Kyle went straight for a vase on the coffee table. Mom whisked it out of reach and put it up on the fireplace mantel.

Kyle turned his attention to ripping pieces off a magazine and putting them in his mouth. Mom moved the magazines. Michael moved the books. Soon all the small, movable objects in the room were on the mantel.

Mrs. Kramer recaptured Kyle and pried the magazine pieces out of his mouth. To keep him under control, she started singing and playing "Itsy Bitsy Spider" with him. That kept him interested about twenty seconds. She switched to peekaboo.

Michael didn't wait to see how long this would keep Kyle occupied. He took his books to his room and closed the door. Far off he heard voices of people arriving and Kyle squealing. Then there was silence. Apparently they had moved into the dining room for the meeting.

He got so interested in reading that he didn't notice how much time had passed. Suddenly Mom came in, lugging Kyle.

"You're going to have to entertain him until we finish the meeting," she said. "It'll only be a few more minutes, but he's driving us all crazy."

"I don't want to," Michael protested.

"Help me with this," she said. "It won't be long." She put Kyle down on Michael's bed. Kyle slid right off and went for the nearest interesting object—Stanley.

Michael herded him out of the room. "No, no," he warned firmly. "Keep your little paws off my plant."

"Let him run out here in the hall," said Mom. She closed the bedroom, bathroom, and kitchen doors. "Don't let him touch anything."

Kyle looked at the closed doors. Then he took off down the hall, squealing in a nerve-racking tone. Michael followed him to the living room. He put Kyle on the couch and tried to interest him with the pictures in another plant book.

"Pretty flowers," said Michael, pointing to a beautiful picture.

"Pitty," agreed Kyle. Then he tried to pick the flowers off the page, crumpling and tearing it.

"No, no," said Michael. While he put the book back on the mantel, Kyle slid off the couch and ran away into the hall. Following, Michael found him on tiptoe, trying to open the bathroom door. Michael pried his tiny fingers from the knob.

"No, no," he repeated. Kyle looked extremely annoyed. He zoomed back to the living room.

Michael went after him. If the meeting wasn't over soon, he thought, he would go crazy. When Michael got to the living room, Kyle disappeared back into the hall. As Michael turned to go after him one more time, Kyle popped back into the room.

"Peekaboo!" said Michael. Kyle chuckled with delight, ran away, and quickly reappeared.

Michael kept yelling, "Peekaboo!" and Kyle kept running in and out. The game was still going on when the dining room door opened and people started leaving.

Kyle appeared in the doorway, grinning. "Peekaboo,'' said Michael one last time. Kyle trotted away again.

"You're so good with him,'' Mrs. Kramer said. "We have an awful time getting sitters. Are you available?''

"No,'' said Michael. He thought he should say something else but didn't know what. There was an awkward silence.

Michael noticed Kyle was taking a long time to come back. What was he doing in the hall?

Howls from that direction sent Michael, Mrs. Kramer, and Mom running. The door to Michael and Norman's room stood ajar. Inside, Kyle, kicking and wiggling, was tightly wrapped in Stanley's vines.

"Hurry!'' yelled Mrs. Kramer. "Get some scissors and cut him loose!''.

"I'll get him out,'' said Michael calmly. "Stand back!'' He carefully unwrapped the vines, muttering quietly to his plant, "Let go, let go. It's OK. I'm helping you.''

Mrs. Kramer thought he was talking to Kyle.

"Hold still, Kyley-Wyley, so Michael can get you loose,'' she said. Kyle cooperated for a change. As Michael freed him from the last vine, he ran into his mother's arms.

She patted him gently. "Isn't it dangerous to have plants that little children can get tangled up in?'' she asked. "He could have gotten accidentally strangled in all those long vines.''

Mom said, "These plants are not recommended for children under three. That's why we kept the door closed. I had no idea he could get it open.''

"Oh, he's very clever about getting into things,'' re-

43

plied Mrs. Kramer. "Aren't you, sweetie pie?" Noticing Kyle's fists were clenched, she pried one open. A crumpled leaf fell out. Out of his other fist fell another leaf. It had been chewed.

"No, no!" exclaimed Mrs. Kramer. "You mustn't put leaves in your mouth."

Michael looked around the room. Leaves were scattered about the floor. He patted Stanley to reassure the plant that the crisis was over.

After Mom saw the Kramers out the front door, she came back to the boys' room.

"Attacking a baby!" she said. "This is the last straw!"

Michael explained, "Stanley didn't attack him! Look at all these leaves he ripped off! Stanley was just defending himself!"

Mom sighed. "Only four more weeks," she said.

Michael didn't want to think about that.

"It's no wonder they have trouble getting babysitters," he said. "They should hire Stanley."

Mom tried not to laugh, but she couldn't help it.

Dad and Norman came home with the news that the Save-A-Lot was sold out of fudge ripple again.

"What's going on?" asked Mom. "Some kind of sudden big fudge ripple fashion thing?"

"Who knows?" replied Dad. "I spoke to the manager. He said they'll be getting more Thursday."

The sun had come out, so the boys rolled the plants outside. That night they put out three socks apiece for the plants, hoping that would be enough after half a day of sun.

Sunday morning Michael woke up when something tickled his nose. It was a soft cloth. Stanley was rubbing it on his face.

44

"Stop that!" he squawked.

"He's dusting," said Norman.

"Not me!" complained Michael. "Do the furniture!"

Norman said, "But you're *on* the furniture."

Fluffy was dusting the headboard of Norman's bed very carefully. Stanley moved on to the lamp on the table between the beds. He dusted it with such enthusiasm that he knocked it off. Crash! Then *schlurrrp!* Stanley ate the dustcloth.

Norman said, "Three socks weren't enough. When I woke up, Fluffy had a vine in my sock drawer. He helped himself to one more."

Michael concluded, "So half a day of sun isn't enough. Hand me my notebook. I have to make research notes."

"Get it yourself," said Norman. "I'm taking Fluffy outside. I think Stanley needs more dusting practice so he doesn't wreck the house."

Chapter 7

At school, kids were having fun mystifying each other with their plants' scientific names.

Chad told Michael and Brad, "Wait till you see my *Crassula argenta*. It's great."

Brad and Michael couldn't guess what that was.

Pat Jenkins told the boys, "I'm bringing a really old *Zygocactus truncatus*."

Michael said, "Obviously it's a cactus."

"Yes," she said, "but bet you don't know what kind of cactus."

None of them did.

Jason would not tell what he was bringing. "Wait and see," he said.

Pat said, "Our creative dramatics class is making up a play about trees."

Michael asked, "What are you going to make the trees out of?"

"We're not making trees," explained Pat. "We're being trees."

Michael couldn't picture this. "How do you be a tree?" he asked.

"It's easy," she said. "You think very hard about being very tall and having bark."

"Oh?" said Michael.

"Yes, your arms are your branches, and your feet are your roots. You stretch out your arms. You feel your roots in the ground. You feel the breeze in your leaves."

Michael said, "You turn on a fan?"

"No! You use your imagination."

"Then what?"

"Then we dance."

"How can you dance when your feet are stuck in the ground?"

Pat replied, "Don't you know anything about creative dramatics?"

"Sure. My brother is dramatic. He put on a show in the garage last summer. He had REAL plants in it."

Pat said, "I have to talk to him. Maybe he can give us some ideas."

"I don't think so," said Michael.

In class they were trying to solve a plant math problem: If a tree grows a ring one-fourth inch wide every year, how old is the tree when it's three feet in diameter?

Everybody got busy.

Michael raised his hand.

"Yes?" said Mrs. Black.

"But trees don't grow the same size rings every year. Some years they're wider or skinnier, depending on the weather. Wouldn't we have to cut the tree down and count the rings to be sure how old it is?"

"You're correct, Michael," she answered. "But this is a tree in a math problem, not a real tree. All the rings in this one are the same just so we can practice our fractions and measurements.''

Michael felt a little silly about having asked this question. He looked down at the floor. Noticing the surrounding feet, he saw that Jason was wearing fudge ripple socks.

''But,'' added Mrs. Black, ''now that you mention it, fortunately there are ways to figure out the ages of trees without cutting them down. Like the two-hundred-year-old oak in the park. We'll have to get more information about how to do that.''

Michael went back to working on the problem.

Mr. Leedy gave Michael a letter to take home about the school district's truck picking up Stanley and Fluffy for Pet Plant Day.

Norman said, ''I wish we could take them in a limo again the way we did for the science fair.''

''They're too big to fit in a limo,'' said Michael. ''That's why we need a truck.''

The letter said the truck would come at 8 A.M. that day. Since the open house for parents was in the evening, Mr. Leedy said the plants would be brought home the next morning.

Dad said, ''Leaving them at school overnight is out of the question. There's no telling what trouble they could get into.''

''Right,'' said Mom. ''I can just picture them rolling up and down the halls or helping themselves to orange juice in the cafeteria refrigerator.''

Norman suggested, ''Or throwing erasers. Or typing on the computers. Or squirting the drinking fountains.''

Dad called Mr. Leedy the next day to tell him the

48

pickup time was fine, but the plants would have to be brought home that night.

Mr. Leedy explained, "The school system won't pay overtime for the truck driver to work at night. But don't worry, the plants will be perfectly safe here."

Dad said he would pay the overtime cost. Mr. Leedy agreed to that.

Dad hung up and remarked to himself with a smile, "Only three more weeks."

Chapter 8

Norman's class started doing creative writing about plants. He was working on his story at the dining room table. Every time Michael walked behind him to peek at what he was writing, Norman covered his papers with his arms.

Michael and Norman kept secretly plugging away at teaching house chores to the plants.

Stanley was getting better at dusting. They ran out of dust in their room, so early in the mornings the boys and the plants sneaked around other rooms to dust quietly.

Fluffy did so well at watering flowers outside with the Blaster that Norman promoted him to using the hose. At first Fluffy kept trying to squeeze the hose the way he squeezed the Blaster trigger. The spray jerked around wildly. Norman got soaked a few times, but he was so pleased with Fluffy's progress that he didn't mind. Fluffy's aim kept improving.

One afternoon Michael decided to ride over to the park to find more kinds of trees for his class tree identification project. Norman insisted on coming along, because he needed more kinds of pinecones for his seed project.

They had been to the park many times with Mom and Dad, but Michael had never noticed how many different kinds of trees there were. Carrying a tree-identification guidebook, he walked his bike into the woods. While he collected a leaf from each new one he found, Norman followed, bossily pointing out trees to him. Michael lost him a few times when he stopped to select pinecones, but he kept catching up. The plastic bag Norman had brought along was almost full of cones.

"Hey, I think that's a ginkgo!" exclaimed Michael. He checked the book to be sure.

"What's that?" asked Norman, running up to see.

"It's a tree," said Michael. "That one." The distinctive fan-shaped leaves were out of reach on the tall tree. He handed the book to Norman, propped his bike against the trunk, and stood up on the seat. But he still couldn't reach a leaf. He climbed down.

"I'll have to find a shorter one," he said.

"I got enough cones," said Norman. "Let's go home."

"I really want one of these leaves," said Michael. "Ginkgos lived in the times of the dinosaurs."

Norman looked amazed. "This tree lived with dinosaurs?"

"Not this exact tree. Other ones just like it."

"Oh," said Norman. "How do you know that?"

"From all the dinosaur books I read. That was before I got interested in plants, so I didn't pay attention to the trees in the pictures. But I always remembered ginkgo because it's such a funny name."

"I'm going to read lots of dinosaur books," said Norman. This made Michael feel irritated. He wanted to be the only dinosaur expert in the family. Norman was always horning in.

"Be careful," warned Michael on the spur of the moment. "Watch out for underground fungus." Norman stopped and glanced at the ground around him.

"There's no such thing here," he said.

"You can't be sure," said Michael. "You can't see something that grows underground. It could be right under your feet, right now, just waiting for some unsuspecting kid to walk on top of it."

Norman started walking faster. "You can't scare me with that," he insisted. "You just made that up! Besides, if it gets me, it gets you, too! Ha, ha!"

Michael lowered his voice. "Be quiet. It might hear you." Norman walked faster. Michael added, "Maybe it's ready to send up some creepy fungus shoots to grab you and pull you down. For lunch!" Norman started jogging.

Michael looked behind him and pretended to see something awful. "Look out!" he yelled.

Norman took off running as if a giant fungus were really after him. Michael stopped because he was laughing so hard.

Although it was only late afternoon, deep shadows darkened these thick woods. Norman had disappeared among the trees. Michael suddenly felt very alone. A creepy feeling came over him. He started running in the direction Norman had gone.

He burst out of the woods. Norman was riding his bike fast down the middle of the empty road. Apparently he had decided that a giant fungus couldn't send up shoots through concrete. Michael hurried after him, staying in the middle of the road, too. He would look for a shorter ginkgo some other time.

A few days later Dr. Sparks called to report several botanical gardens wanted to buy Stanley and Fluffy, because they were the biggest and best ones of the so-far-unidentified species. Two wanted to display them eating socks, because that would be a sensational attraction that the gardens could sell tickets for.

Mom said, "But not many people are going to buy tickets for something that happens in the middle of the night."

Dr. Sparks replied, "Their light cycle can be changed so they'll eat at a more convenient time—the way we've done with the small ones we're experimenting with here."

She told Mom the gardens would be sending them offers and information to look over before they decided which one to sell the plants to.

Norman and Michael were upset at the news that the botanical garden plan was progressing.

"Our house-chore plan better work," said Norman. "It will work, won't it?"

"Calm down," said Michael, who was not feeling very calm himself. "It's bound to make them change their minds. We should be ready to show them soon. But the plants still need more practice."

"How much time do we have left?" asked Norman.

Michael went and looked at the calendar.

"Only two more weeks," he said.

Chapter 9

Ever since Michael had noticed Jason wearing fudge ripple socks one day, he found he kept glancing at Jason's socks. Day after day they were fudge ripple.

But that didn't prove anything, Michael thought. He and Norman had looked all over Jason's house in July after Mom spotted Jason buying a bunch of strawberry socks at the Save-A-Lot. His suspicion that Jason might have kept one baby plant had come to nothing.

On her next trip to the Save-A-Lot, Mom came home with a good supply of fudge ripple.

"Goody," said Norman. "Fluffy will be happy."

Mom remarked, "There were plenty of these on the shelf. I guess whoever was buying them up doesn't need any more."

A couple of days later, Michael noticed that Jason was wearing blue socks. The next day he was wearing gray. These two colors were definitely not delicious to sock-eating plants.

But Michael couldn't stop wondering why Jason had worn fudge ripple every day for a long time and then

54

stopped. So when Jason mentioned that he had bought a new video game, Michael invited himself over that day after school to see it.

Jason didn't look enthusiastic, but he said, "OK."

It was Wednesday, when Mom wouldn't be home until later, so Michael found Norman right after school and told him where he was going.

"I'm just going to take one more look around," he said. "I'll be home soon. Have you got your key?"

"Of course," said Norman. "But I can come with you."

"No," said Michael. He didn't want his little brother tagging along. "It'll look suspicious if we both go again. I'll be home before Mom gets back."

Michael unlocked his bike and rode along home with Jason. After one quick video game, he asked for a drink of water so he could visit the kitchen, and made a trip to the bathroom so he could see the upstairs rooms. Then Michael said he had to be going. He hadn't seen a single plant in the whole place.

Jason didn't urge him to stay for another game. As Michael was leaving, Jason's mother said they had to do some errands. Michael was a little way down the block when their car passed him. They waved.

He was halfway home when a thought struck him. If there wasn't even one plant there, what was Jason going to bring to Pet Plant Day?

There had to be one there somewhere. And if it wasn't in the house, where was it? He decided to ride back and check the garage.

He felt nervous about sneaking on somebody else's property. He glanced about to see if anyone might be

55

watching. A tall, thick hedge stood across the back of the yard, so no one could see from that direction.

The garage door was locked. He went around to one side and found a window.

Peering into the dim garage, he didn't see any plants. But a pile of boxes blocked his view of the other side. He decided to go around and peek in the window on that side. Rather than leave his bike in front of the garage, he rolled it along to leave it in back, out of sight in case anybody came while he checked the other window.

As he turned the corner in back of the garage, he came face-to-face—or rather, face-to-leaves—with what he was looking for, Jason's secret plant.

There, in the narrow space between the back of the garage and the hedge, growing in deep shade, the plant, about four feet tall, stood rooted in the ground. It was the same kind as Stanley and Fluffy. Jason had kept one after all.

Although Michael felt angry at Jason, he was interested to see another one of these plants.

Because he was used to talking to his own, he said, "So you must eat dirty socks just like Stanley."

He stepped up to get a closer look. This one didn't look as healthy as Stanley and Fluffy. He felt something on his ankle and looked down. A vine was curling around his fudge ripple sock.

"Oh, you like fudge ripple, do you?" he said. The vine tightened its grip.

"Let go," he said. But this wasn't Stanley, who understood "Hang on" and "Let go."

Before Michael could bend down to free his ankle, the plant whirled all its vines so fast that Michael was wrapped in an iron grip before he realized what was happening.

His arms were tightly held to his sides so he couldn't use his hands to try to get loose. His legs were wrapped, too. Now he knew how Kyle must have felt. But he hadn't done anything to annoy this plant.

"This is ridiculous," he said. "Let me go. I'm a friend."

The plant tightened its hold.

Michael was astonished at how strong this plant was, and how unfriendly. The way it was clutching him, he couldn't use his strength to break vines or lean forward to pull the plant out of the ground. He tried, but nothing worked. He was stuck, a prisoner.

He felt vines pulling his shoes off, and then his socks. That's what it wants, he thought. Now it will let go.

The plant used one vine to quickly feed itself the two socks. But it didn't release him. Michael was beginning to get the feeling that it just didn't like him.

It's going to be really embarrassing, he thought, if anybody finds me here. Then he thought, what if *nobody* finds me here?

He started yelling, "Help! Help! Is anybody there? Help! Behind the garage!"

This seemed to annoy the plant further. As he opened his mouth to yell again, it shoved a bunch of leaves in. That muffled his call of "Help" so it sounded more like a quiet "Murmph." Nobody could hear him now unless someone happened to come very close.

Michael stopped struggling while he tried to think of what to do next. Surely he could outthink a plant.

If he could only reach his pocket knife, he could cut his way out. But he could barely wiggle his fingers.

Time passed. His arms and legs began to feel stiff. Every once in a while he mumbled, "Murmph," but nobody came.

After a long time, he heard a car. At last! Jason would get him out of this. The garage door rolled up on its tracks. The car drove in and shut off. He kept mumbling, "Murmph, murmph," as loud as he could. But they didn't hear him. The garage door went back down. Then the back door of the house slammed.

Maybe Jason will come out to feed the plant, Michael thought. But Jason didn't come.

When I don't come home, Michael thought, Norman will tell them where I went, and Mom and Dad will come looking. But Jason's mom will tell them I left hours ago. And they won't look behind the garage.

More time passed. The plant didn't relax its hold. Michael wondered why this one was so mean. It was not at all like Stanley and Fluffy. He thought it must be getting late. It would be getting dark soon.

A long time later he heard a funny noise and realized it was familiar. What he heard somewhere nearby was *swoosh, swoosh, swoosh, swoosh.*

"Murmph, Murmph," Michael mumbled as loudly as he could. The *swoosh*es stopped. He kept making noises. Then the *swoosh*ing speeded up, and Norman came around the back of the garage.

He saw immediately that Michael had a mouthful of leaves, so he scooped them out. The plant slapped his hand, and he jumped back away from it.

"Careful," warned Michael. "It's Stanley's evil twin."

"Okay," said Norman. "But I don't have anything to cut the vines with."

"My knife's in my right pocket," said Michael. "Grab it fast, so this monster doesn't get you, too."

Norman looked the situation over. "It doesn't have enough vines," he concluded, "to hold both of us."

"Good thinking," said Michael. "Go for it whenever you're ready, but hurry up!"

Norman darted forward and reached into the pocket. A vine grabbed his wrist, but he pulled hard the other way and got free with the knife.

"Don't just get the ends," said Michael. "Cut as near the stalk as you can."

Norman darted back and forth between cuts. As each vine was cut, it went limp. Michael soon was able to pull free. He stretched his arms and legs. Then he sat down far from the plant and put on his shoes.

"Thank goodness you found me," he said. "What took you so long?"

"You've only been gone about an hour," said Norman.

Michael looked at his watch. Norman was right. But it had seemed like hours and hours.

"Then why did you come here?"

"I wanted to know what was happening. So I rode my bike over and went to the door. Jason said you left before they went to do errands. But if you were on your way home already, I would have passed you on my way over here. So I sort of wondered. Besides, I wanted to peek in the garage in case he had a plant in there. That's when I heard you making funny noises. Except I didn't know it was you. What do you

59

think is wrong with this plant? It's dangerous. Maybe we should cut it down.''

Michael replied, "Not until we ask Jason what's wrong with it. It might be scientific evidence. We should tell Dr. Sparks.''

Norman asked, "You're going to tell Jason you found his plant?''

"Am I ever!'' said Michael. "Right now!''

"But then he'll know we sneaked around his garage,'' said Norman. "Maybe we should just go home.''

Michael said, "Him sneaking a plant was a bigger sneak than our sneaks. Follow me!''

He marched to the back door and rang the bell.

When Jason opened the door, Michael unwound a leftover piece of vine from his arm and threw it at him.

"What about this plant!'' he yelled.

"What plant?'' replied Jason, looking guilty.

"The one behind the garage!''

Jason stepped out into the yard and closed the door behind him.

"Oh,'' he said quietly. "You found it.''

Michael said angrily, "You told me you gave us back all the baby plants!''

Jason replied, "I said all the ones I sold. I didn't sell this one. I kept it 'cause I wanted a great plant like yours. There wasn't any other way to get one. I was going to dig it up in time to take it to Pet Plant Day, but it started acting terrible. It got out of control.''

Norman exclaimed, "It's a monster!''

Michael said, "It won't be out of control anymore. We just cut the vines off.''

"I did that, too,'' said Jason, "all except one so it

60

could feed itself. But they grew back real fast, stronger than before. And it was finally up to six socks a night. It didn't care whether they were clean or dirty. Just so they were white with brown stripes. I don't know why. It used to like pink ones, but when I gave it other colors, it started throwing them back at me. I was running out of money even though I sold a lot of my stuff. So I stopped feeding it a week ago. I hope it'll starve."

"Why didn't you cut it down?" asked Michael.

"It wouldn't let me," explained Jason. "Any time I got close enough to try, it grabbed at me. That is one mean plant!"

"You should get a skunk," suggested Norman.

"What did your mom say about it?" asked Michael.

"She never goes in back of the garage," said Jason. "That's why I planted it there."

"Why didn't you tell me?" asked Michael.

"I knew you'd be mad," said Jason. "I thought about telling you lots of times, but I kept putting it off."

Michael stood silently for a moment. Then his curiosity took over. "Why does your plant act that way?" he asked. "It's from one of Stanley's seeds, but it's not anything like my plant."

Jason shrugged. "Must have been a bad seed," he said. "It never liked me."

"How did you raise it?" asked Michael.

"I threw some socks out there every night before I went to bed. I let the rain water it."

Norman frowned at Jason. "Did you talk to it?" he asked.

"Nope."

"Did you sing to it?"

"Of course not!"

"Did you keep it company so it didn't get lonesome?"

"No."

"Then there's your problem!" deduced Norman.

Michael agreed. "We raised our plants with a lot of attention. Maybe the way you neglected it made the difference."

"That's silly," said Jason. "But it doesn't matter now."

Michael said, "I'm going to tell the botanist we know about this."

Jason looked alarmed. "I don't want my mother to find out," he said. "She said I couldn't keep even one baby plant, so I sort of let her think I gave them *all* back to you. I'd be in big trouble."

Michael thought it would serve him right, but he didn't say so.

"We better go home," said Norman. As they picked up their bikes to leave, Michael remarked to Jason, "So you're not bringing anything to Pet Plant Day."

"Yes, I am," said Jason. "My uncle told me about a place that rents big plants to buildings. He's going to help me rent a huge rubber plant just for that day. A six-feet-tall one. It's going to be great. Uncle Jim's going to pick it up from them and deliver it to school."

"No fair," said Norman. "You're supposed to bring a plant you took care of yourself."

"I'm paying for it myself," said Jason. "My uncle's giving me the money, but I'm paying him back."

Michael asked, "What happened to that snake plant you got for a pet plant last spring? The one you called Fang."

"I don't know. I left it in the garage a long time ago. It must still be there behind some piles of stuff. It's dead by now." He went back in his house and closed the door.

Norman said, "He shouldn't be allowed to have any plants!"

"You got that right," agreed Michael.

As they pedaled homeward, Norman said, "Mom and Dad are going to be upset when we tell them about Jason's plant."

Michael replied, "Let's wait a few days—until after we get them to change their minds about Stanley and Fluffy."

Chapter 10

Before dinner that evening, the boys got into an argument about whose turn it was to set the table. Mom settled the issue by making them both do it.

When Dad got home a few minutes later, Norman was bossily telling Michael that the forks were supposed to go on top of the napkins, not next to them. Michael ignored him, so Norman went around the table and moved all the forks. Michael didn't care where the forks were, but he wouldn't let Norman win. He moved them back. Norman whined to Mom about it.

She replied firmly, "Sit down and be quiet. We're ready to eat."

They sat quietly while Dad said a blessing. Then Michael put his fork on top of his napkin and yanked the napkin off the table. The fork flipped off and hit the floor with a clank.

"See?" he told Norman.

Norman glared at him.

Dad and Mom hardly ever took sides in their arguments, although the boys both tried to get them to. This time Dad just changed the subject.

"Let's go to the library tonight," he said. "I've got an overdue book, and I need to look some stuff up."

At the library, Michael photocopied his scientific notes to mail to Dr. Sparks. While he was looking for plant books, he found a great dinosaur book, one he had never seen before. The beautifully painted pictures showed dinosaurs in their natural world. The trees and other plants looked interesting. He checked it out so Norman couldn't get it first.

In the car, Norman beat him to the front seat, so Michael sat in back with all the books. As they drove along, there was enough light from streetlights to see pictures. He started leafing through the dinosaur book, looking at the plants.

He remarked to Dad, "Lots of plants are alive today that lived with the dinosaurs. Here's a ginkgo tree." From reading so many plant books, he could now recognize many others, although they weren't identified.

"Here's a magnolia," he continued. "Cycads—they look like palm trees, but they're not related." He kept turning pages. "Horsetails . . . club mosses . . . lots of ferns . . . HOLY COW!"

Norman asked in an amazed tone, "A plant that looks like a cow?"

"No!" yelled Michael. "One of the prehistoric plants in this book looks a lot like Stanley and Fluffy!"

Dad hit the brakes and pulled into a parking space. Michael handed the book into the front seat.

"Wow!" exclaimed Norman. "It's taller than that apatosaurus there! Do you think ours will grow that big?"

Dad said, "It *does* look like them!"

"Yay!" shouted Norman. "Fluffy's prehistoric. This is great! Now we can be on TV again and keep our plants!"

"Hold on," said Dad. "We don't know whether this artist was using scientific evidence or his imagination or some of both."

"Yeah," said Michael. "Some dinosaur bones turned out to be put together wrong. Sometimes scientists guess if they don't find the whole thing. It could be that way with plants, too."

Dad asked, "Did you ever see a plant like that in any other dinosaur book you read?"

"I don't think so. But I was only interested in the dinosaurs then, not plants."

"When was the book published?" asked Dad. "Look on the back of the title page and see what the copyright date is."

Michael grabbed the book back from Norman to check. "It's this year," he said.

Dad pulled out of the parking space, heading for home. "We're going to call whoever painted those pictures and wrote the book," he said.

"What about Dr. Sparks?" asked Michael.

"We'll call her, too."

As they passed under the next streetlight, Michael looked at the flap of the book cover. The author was Ramon J. Spondoolick, Ph.D., a professor of paleontology at Rockville University in Colorado. The illustrator was Barnaby J. Millerkin, who lived in Hanover, New Hampshire.

Mom was flabbergasted at the picture. "But it doesn't look exactly like ours," she pointed out. "The shape and the vines do, but the rolled-up leaves are not as ice-cream-cone-shaped as Stanley and Fluffy's.''

Norman explained, ''That's because dinosaurs didn't have ice cream cones. So the leaves didn't know how to look like that.''

''Yours never were around ice cream cones either,'' said Mom. ''These in the book look more like cardboard tubes from toilet paper.''

''Dinosaurs didn't have toilet paper either,'' said Norman. ''And what did those plants eat? Dinosaurs didn't have socks!''

He thought a minute. ''Hey!'' he exclaimed. ''Maybe this shows that dinosaurs did have socks and toilet paper!''

Michael shook his head in disbelief.

By now Dad had called information and gotten the home phone numbers of the author and illustrator. First he tried Millerkin, but there was no answer. The boys were listening on the extension in their parents' bedroom. They kept bumping heads, but they were too excited to get irritated at each other.

Next Dad tried the paleontologist. On the second ring he got Mrs. Spondoolick. But her husband wasn't home. ''He's on a dig in Mongolia,'' she said. ''He'll be back in a couple of months. Can I take a message? Or maybe someone at his office can help you tomorrow.''

Dad said, ''I'll try to keep calling Barnaby Millerkin. He can probably answer my question.''

''But he's in Mongolia, too,'' said Mrs. Spondoolick, ''doing drawings for a book on the dig.''

''What I'm calling about,'' said Dad, ''is something in your husband's new book. On page fourteen, the funny-looking third plant from the left. Would you happen to know if this picture is scientifically accurate or the artist's idea?''

"I don't know," she replied. "But my husband always gives artists a hard time about getting things right. Although sometimes, when paleontologists have fossil evidence of only small parts of something newly discovered, they try to reconstruct what the whole thing was like. Sometimes they guess wrong.''

"Would you ask Dr. Spondoolick about this when he calls home?''

"Certainly," she said. "He'll be calling in two and a half weeks. He has to trek a hundred and forty miles to the nearest phone." Dad gave her their phone number and thanked her.

Mom volunteered to call Dr. Sparks. "I have a very strange question about the plants," she began. "Promise you won't laugh.''

"OK," said Dr. Sparks. "Are they doing something else unusual?''

"This is beyond our wildest imaginings," said Mom. She explained about the picture. "And the author and illustrator can't be reached for two and a half weeks. Of course, this is so farfetched, but—''

Dr. Sparks interrupted excitedly. "Unlikely does not mean impossible," she said. "Many plants living today also existed in the dinosaur eras.''

Michael asked, "But could our plants be like that?''

She replied, "When I studied for my degrees, there were no known fossil plants like these. But I don't keep up with paleobotany. I'll check with the paleobotanist at the natural history museum first thing in the morning. He'll know about any recent fossil discoveries.''

Norman asked, "Do you think Fluffy is extinct?"

She replied, "Since he's alive, he can't be extinct. But sometimes plants and animals that scientists knew only from fossils have been found alive—even though everyone thought they died out millions of years ago."

"Wow!" said Norman, awed at this news. "Then maybe there's still a few dinosaurs left."

Dr. Sparks chuckled. "If there were, I think someone would have noticed them by now.

"But then," she added, "there was a fish, the coelacanth, that everyone thought had died out five million years ago. Then somebody caught a live one off the coast of Africa in 1934. That was a big surprise!"

Michael asked, "What kind of plants got found?"

Dr. Sparks said, "There were strange trees discovered in a remote area of China in 1944. When they were finally identified, they turned out to be dawn redwoods, which used to be a favorite dinosaur dinner."

Michael asked, "What happened to the three trees?"

"I don't know. But botanists shared the seeds. Now dawn redwoods grow all over the world."

"It would be great if our plants turn out to be like that," he said.

"It would be thrilling," said Dr. Sparks. "I'll call you the minute I have any news."

After they hung up, Michael said, "Now this means we can keep our plants, right?"

"Wrong," said Dad.

"But why not? They might be scientific wonders!"

"That doesn't make them cheaper to feed or easier to take care of. It's all the more reason why they should be safely in the care of scientists."

69

Norman protested, "But we take good care of them. And some nights they're only eating three socks apiece. That's cheaper."

Mom pointed out, "That's because they're getting more sunlight. Soon the weather will be too cold for them to sit outside. Then they'll be back to four socks and maybe more. The bigger they get, the more they eat. And we don't know how big they'll grow."

Chapter 11

When Dr. Sparks called back the next afternoon, she was very excited.

"There are some recently discovered unidentified fossils," she said. "They were found in Asia within the last year. The paleobotanist I talked to at the museum had pictures of them. They look like your plants, only much bigger. Was he ever surprised when I told him we had some live ones. The artist who did the pictures for that dinosaur book must have known about the fossils."

"Wow!" said Norman, who was listening with Michael on the bedroom phone.

"This is great!" said Michael. "But how come hardly anybody knows about those fossils?"

"Paleobotanists know," she replied, "because they share information all the time. The fossils are being studied in Asia, but research takes a lot of time because it's done very carefully."

"When is this going to be on TV?" asked Norman.

"Not for a long time. Many months, maybe even years," said Dr. Sparks. Norman was disappointed. He wanted to be on TV with his plant again.

"Why does it take so long?" he asked.

"Science moves slowly," explained Dr. Sparks. "First, experts work together to do the research and share their information with other experts. Then they write an article about what they've done for a scientific journal. If the journal publishes the article, then it might be reported on TV and in the newspapers. It doesn't work like in the movies, where somebody looks through a microscope, says, 'Aha!' and bam! It's sensational worldwide news."

Michael said, "Can't we tell anybody?"

"I wouldn't say too much until the plants are safely settled in a botanical garden," said Dr. Sparks. "Unless you want people sneakily picking leaves off your plants for souvenirs until there aren't any left, it would be better just to say that they might be Paleolithic survivors, but scientists haven't confirmed it yet."

Mom asked, "Does this mean our plants will be worth more money?"

"Oh, yes," said Dr. Sparks. "And any seeds you have will be worth more, too. I'm packing up some of the smaller plants to send to researchers this week. I wish I could talk to your Dr. Spondoolick to see if he knows anything more than I've found out."

"That's a great idea," said Mom, giving Dr. Sparks the Spondoolicks' phone number. "Now you can arrange it so *you* get a long distance call from Mongolia in the middle of the night, not us."

Michael thought it would be fun to get a long distance call from Mongolia, but he didn't say anything.

When they got off the phone, Michael told Mom, "Now we have to keep these plants."

"No," she said, "they're too valuable. That's just one more reason why not."

Michael replied, "But when the ones Dr. Sparks has get bigger and grow seed pods, there'll be lots more plants and more pods. When there are thousands of plants in a few years, ours won't be valuable anymore because they won't be rare."

Mom replied, "Michael, we've been over this so many times. We can't keep the plants. You know that's final. I'm sorry. I know how much you care about Stanley." She gave him a hug.

As the boys were going to bed, Norman asked Michael, "Do you think Fluffy was dinosaur dinner?"

"Could be," said Michael. "But not actually Fluffy. His Paleolithic ancestors. Maybe when they grew as big as in that picture in the book, their vines were so big and strong that they could push dinosaurs away. Or trip them. Or wrap them up and hold them tight until they gave up."

Norman asked, "But what do you think they ate if dinosaurs didn't wear socks?"

"Who knows? Trees maybe. Or flowers."

"Would plants eat other plants?" wondered Norman.

"Maybe," said Michael. "Some dinosaurs used to eat other dinosaurs."

"Oh, yuck," said Norman.

Early one morning after an hour of dusting and high-shelf-reaching practice with the plants, Michael said, "I think we're almost ready to show Dad and Mom. Just a few more days of practice."

"Yeah," agreed Norman. "Fluffy only knocked over one chair dusting today. Pretty soon, he won't be knocking anything over."

Michael added, "And Stanley's doing great on lifting and lowering cans from the highest kitchen shelves that Mom can't reach. He only dropped two today."

At breakfast Dad announced, "Only one more week to Pet Plant Day. We have to make up our minds now about which botanical garden to sell the plants to."

"I don't want to talk about it," said Norman.

Mom said, "This has to be a family decision that both of you are in on. They're your plants."

Michael replied, "I don't want to talk about it, either."

"Make up your minds that you have to talk about it," said Mom firmly. "Here's the deal. We can choose the one that's offering the most money. That would be the sensible choice. Or the one that's closest, so we can go visit once in a while."

"Closest," said the boys in unison.

"OK," said Dad. "I'll call that one today to tell them yes."

Michael asked, just out of curiosity, since it wasn't going to matter anyway, "How close is it?"

"About five or six hundred miles," answered Dad. "Maybe an eleven- or twelve-hour drive, depending on how many times we stop to eat. We can probably go once or twice a year."

That would be terrible, Michael thought. It was a good thing the plants wouldn't be going.

After breakfast, he told Norman, "Don't worry. As soon as we change their minds, Dad'll have to call that

74

garden back and tell them Stanley and Fluffy aren't coming."

In the kitchen Dad remarked to Mom, "They're taking this a lot better than I expected."

The botanical garden director told Dad that he would send a heated truck to pick up the plants. A botanist would come along to take care of them on the way. The date was set for ten days after Pet Plant Day. Michael and Norman were glad to have a little more time for house-chore practice. They decided to try to be ready the day after Pet Plant Day.

Now that Mom thought the plants were all set to be going far, far away, she stopped complaining about the cost of socks to feed them and all the problems they caused. She didn't get very annoyed even when Stanley got hold of a green marker Michael had carelessly left within reach and scribbled all over the wall beside his bed and his bedspread. She even helped the boys clean up the mess.

"Boy, is she ever in a good mood!" exclaimed Norman.

She was singing quietly to herself, "Only fourteen more days, only fourteen more days."

Chapter 12

The night before Pet Plant Day, the boys washed and polished the plants' leaves. Norman wanted to put a bow on Fluffy, but Mom talked him out of it.

After dinner Norman announced that he was ready to read his story.

"This better be good," grumbled Michael.

"It is good," snapped Norman. He cleared his throat and began.

"A green alien flew to Earth for vacation," he read. "He had leaves for hair. He had roots for feet. He landed his spaceship. It looked like an RV, only bigger.

"He went to Disney World. His roots were cold, so he bought socks. He got lost in a swamp at night. He escaped from alligators and a swamp monster."

Michael commented, "This is the story of our Florida vacation."

"No, it's not," replied Norman. "I made it up."

He continued, "The alien went to the post office. He sent a postcard to his grandmother. He wrote her he was having a good time."

Michael said, "You can't mail postcards to other planets."

Norman said, "In creative writing you can do anything." He read on. "The alien lost two seeds from his pocket. They fell in a letter for a boy named Norman. Then the alien reached in his pocket. He found the keys to his spaceship. He could not find his lost seeds. He looked all over, but he had to go home. He flew away. He hoped his seeds were found by an Earthling who would take good care of them. The end."

Michael said, "He's going to get home before his postcard does."

Mom said, "That's an excellent story."

Dad said, "You did a wonderful job. That was really interesting. It does sound like our vacation."

"That was my inspiration," said Norman. He showed everyone the pictures he had drawn with the story. The last one showed a boy who looked a little like Norman taking care of two big plants that looked a lot like Fluffy and Stanley.

"Excellent artwork," said Dad.

"Where am I in this picture?" asked Michael. "One of the plants is mine."

"You're not in the story," said Norman.

"You have to put me in," said Michael.

"No, I don't," replied Norman. "This is creative writing."

In the morning, Mom came along with the boys in the back of the truck. Norman had insisted on riding there to make sure Fluffy would not get upset. They helped the driver take the plants in. He gave Mom a ride home in the front seat.

A traffic jam was starting in front of the school. More parents than usual were driving kids who usually walked because they were carrying plants. The yellow buses unloaded their riders more slowly than usual because they were lugging plants, too.

Mr. Leedy and Mr. Jones were directing traffic along with the crossing guards. Some teachers came out to help the smallest children.

Michael stood in the front hallway watching the parade of plants—big, little, and middle-sized. Jason and his large rented one had not arrived yet.

He went on back to their room. Jason finally came in carrying a plastic grocery bag.

"What happened to your six-foot plant?" asked Michael.

Jason looked irritated.

"My uncle Jim read about Pet Plant Day in the newspaper. He found out we were supposed to bring our own plants that we took care of. He said it wouldn't be right to rent one. So he decided not to lend me the money."

"What's in the bag?" asked Michael. Jason opened it and took out a pathetic snake plant. The spear-shaped leaves were dusty. Some were wrinkled at the bottom and dried up. But some looked OK.

"Is that Fang?" asked Michael.

"Yeah, good thing it didn't die after all. I looked snake plants up in a book at the library last night for my report. It said they can keep going for months with total neglect."

"Perfect for you," said Michael. "Maybe you better wipe the dust off before your presentation."

"The PA system interrupted to settle the classroom

down with the pledge of allegiance. Then Norman's voice came from the box on the wall.

"A poem," he said. "Hip, hip, hooray. Today is Pet Plant Day. We're learning about growing. So lots we are knowing. Pet plants are our friends. I hope Pet Plant Day never ends. The end."

Michael thought the poem was dumb, but Pat Jenkins said, "That was a nice poem." Well, at least he didn't sing it, Michael thought.

The class started their presentations.

Kimberly Offenberg showed the three kinds of philodendron she had grown from cuttings. She also showed color slides she had taken at different stages.

Another girl explained that her prayer plant was named that because it folded up its leaves at night. Of course, since it was day now, the leaves did not fold up. So she showed a picture of that.

Pat Jenkins announced, "This is my *Zygocactus truncatus,* also known as the Christmas cactus. These plants originally came from the mountain forests of Brazil in South America. I got this one from my grandmother. Somebody gave it to her when she got married forty-two years ago. She doesn't know how old it was then, but it wasn't very big."

Michael was amazed to see a forty-two-year-old houseplant.

Pat went on at great length about how it would bloom with bright pink flowers in November. But it wouldn't bloom unless it got enough hours of darkness. She showed a picture in a book of a Christmas cactus in bloom. It was spectacular.

Chad Palmer presented his *Crassula argenta,* a jade plant. The plump oval leaves looked padded. He explained that it was a succulent originally from South Africa. "I bought it at the Save-A-Lot last spring," he said. "You're not supposed to water succulents very often. It's easy to take care of."

Brad Chan told how his poinsettia, also known as *Euphorbia pulcherrima,* was named after Dr. Joel Poinsett. He brought the plants to America from Mexico in 1828. "In very warm countries," said Brad, "they grow outside like shrubbery, up to ten feet tall."

Michael tried to picture a row of poinsettia bushes four feet taller than Stanley.

Brad explained how the red leaves were not flowers. They were called bracts. Their color attracted insects to the real flower parts, the little yellow thingies in the center. The bracts wouldn't turn red unless the plants got long hours of darkness, like Pat's cactus.

Others showed plants they had grown from a sweet potato, an avocado seed, and the top cut from a pineapple. There was a spider plant with little planlets hanging down from it. There were Swedish ivy, English ivy, and grape ivy.

Then it was Michael's turn. He told how no one knew what kind Stanley was, but botanists were working on finding out. The class looked impressed. He told about how he had grown Stanley from a seed and taken him on vacation. Then he showed the picture in the dinosaur book. People began to mutter things like "That really looks like it" and "It's a dinosaur plant." It was a sensation.

"That's astounding," said Mrs. Black. "Now, settle down, class. I'm sure Michael will tell us as soon as the scientists let him know. We mustn't jump to conclusions. It's a fascinating theory, but we don't know for sure yet."

Next it was Jason's turn. He stood up with poor Fang, still dusty. "This is *Sansevieria,* called the snake plant," he said. "This is a plant you don't have to take care of. I bought it last spring. Then I put it in the garage all summer and let it go without water. This week I brought it back in the house and watered it. So this shows how long a snake plant can go without water without dying."

Mrs. Black said, "Very interesting, Jason. You certainly have an unusual angle there. But I'm sure that plant would do better if it were taken care of. You are going to take care of it from now on, aren't you?"

"Sure," said Jason. "Now that my experiment is over."

Then Mrs. Black brought out her plant. "This is *Mimosa pudica,*" she said, "also known as sensitive plant. Can you guess why?"

Somebody called out, "It gets its feelings hurt easily?" Everybody laughed.

"That's a good guess. I'll give you another hint. It's also called the shy plant."

"It's afraid to talk to people?" suggested Michael. Mrs. Black laughed along with everyone else.

"If it could talk," she replied, "it probably would be too shy to speak up. Now I'll show you why it's called sensitive and shy. I need a volunteer." From the waving hands, she chose Pat and told everyone to gather around so they could see.

"Just touch the leaves gently," Mrs. Black instructed. The instant Pat touched the plant, the leaves closed.

Everyone said, "Ooh," because they were so surprised.

Chapter 13

Soon it was time to take their plants to the gym. While other placed theirs on tables and shelves set up on the gym floor, Michael rolled Stanley to the far end where the stage was. Fluffy was already up there. Mr. Jones came over.

"These sure have grown since the science fair last spring," he remarked. "Mr. Leedy decided this morning that they're too big for the special platform I built. So they're going to just stand on the stage floor." He got a couple of other boys to help him and Michael hoist Stanley up over the edge of the stage.

Michael went up the steps at the side and rolled Stanley next to Fluffy. On the wall behind them was a huge sign painted by the art classes. It said, WELCOME TO PET PLANT DAY.

A podium and microphone stood nearby.

Mr. Jones said, "Stand over there by the podium so I can see how the lights look on that spot." Michael moved over there. "That's it," said Mr. Jones. He stepped into the dark space at one side. Michael heard switches being flipped—thunk, thunk, thunk. Bright lights hit him.

"How does that look from there?" called Mr. Jones.

When Michael answered, "Looks good from here," his voice boomed off the gym walls.

"Oops," said Mr. Jones, "I turned on the mike switch by mistake." Michael heard another thunk.

Mrs. Black called up from the gym floor, "He needs more light on his face. He looks like he's holding a flashlight under his chin for Halloween."

Mr. Jones made Michael stay put while he focused lights and went back and forth to see how they looked from the gym floor. Then he focused lights on Fluffy and Stanley.

"All set," Mr. Jones finally said. "See you tonight."

Michael went down the stage steps to go back to his room. At the gym door, he glanced back. Stanley and Fluffy looked calm and content. Mr. Jones turned out the stage lights. Michael went on his way.

Just as school was letting out, Mom arrived. She was all dressed up and carrying a picnic cooler. "We're eating dinner here," she said. "In the gym. Just to be sure nothing goes wrong with the plants."

"Does Mr. Leedy know about this?" asked Michael.

"Yes, I told him our family would stay here in case any unexpected last-minute things needed to be done for the open house. He said that will be fine. He and Mr. Jones would be here, except when they go home for dinner. I told him I'd stay in the office in case there were any last minute phone calls."

Norman asked, "But what are we supposed to do?"

"One of you stay in the gym at all times," she said.

Later when Dad came, the family had a picnic dinner in the gym.

To Michael's surprise, Mr. Jones closed the stage curtains and put the mike stand in front of them.

"Mr. Leedy thinks this is a good idea," Mr. Jones told the family. "This way, when I open the curtain, it'll be a sort of a ta-da thing, very dramatic."

Michael hoped that the plants wouldn't start acting up if it was dark backstage. He went up behind the curtains a few times to check. The plants were not stirring.

By seven o'clock, the school was swarming with people. Children were proudly taking their families around to show off their plant unit work. Parents were taking pictures all over the place. Up and down the halls, students pointed out their "favorite book" leaves on the vines along the walls.

Michael kept glancing at the stage, wondering when Mr. Leedy was going to open the curtains. Finally Mr. Leedy went up the stage steps to the mike. He tapped on it to see if it was on. It wasn't, so he started trying to find where the curtains divided. He finally found the right spot and stuck his head in to tell Mr. Jones to hit the switch. Mr. Leedy tapped the mike again. This time everyone heard the loud thump it made. The crowd quieted down to listen.

"Welcome to Pet Plant Day," Mr. Leedy announced. "I want to congratulate and thank everyone who helped make this such a success." He called many people up onstage, one by one, for special recognition. He thanked the students, the teachers, the parents, the librarian, and the school secretary.

"And last, but not least," he added, "a person we could not run this school without. Mr. Jones did the whole setup for this exhibit in addition to all his other duties. Mr. Jones, come out and take a bow!"

The curtains thrashed. Mr. Jones's head popped out. People applauded. His head vanished.

"And now," said Mr. Leedy, "the family that started this whole thing!" Norman eagerly bounded up the steps. Dad, Mom, and Michael followed.

"As most of you recall," continued Mr. Leedy, "Michael brought two unusual plants to the science fair last spring. And when Norman's class wrote letters to the newspaper, his letter about how plants make good pets got published. That led to TV news coverage, and the pet plant idea spread."

He turned to Mom and Dad. "We have this engraved plaque for you because you encouraged your sons' interest in plants. You set a good example for all the parents in our community. You made room in your home and your hearts for those two large green adopted members of your family. Thank you and congratulations." He handed the plaque to Mom, who thanked him.

"And now," announced Mr. Leedy, "tonight is our last chance to see the plants that started it all. They're making their last public appearance in our town tonight. In ten days they're going to a famous botanical garden to live and be studied because they're so rare.

"And now here are our green guests of honor," said Mr. Leedy. He pointed to the curtains with a sweep of his arm, but they didn't open. From between them reached a leafy vine! The crowd laughed.

"Jones," muttered Mr. Leedy to the curtain, "quit fooling around. This is no time for plant jokes! Just open the curtains!"

Michael grabbed the vine and plunged through the curtains, colliding with Stanley on the other side. The plant had rolled forward and was waving vines around.

Fluffy was clutching the podium and looked ready to roll. Mr. Jones was off to the side by the switches, where he had just turned on the stage lights. He looked amazed, as if he had seen a ghost.

Michael peeked out between the curtains, grabbed Norman by the back of his belt, and yanked him backstage. When Norman vanished, Mr. Leedy looked startled. Dad and Mom were still looking out at the audience, so they didn't notice the commotion.

Norman untangled Fluffy from the podium and shoved him sideways. Michael put Stanley back next to Fluffy. He told Mr. Jones, "You can open the curtain now."

The custodian pulled the rope. The curtains parted, showing the boys holding on to their plants' main stalks. One of Stanley's vines was around Michael's shoulder.

"And here they are!" exclaimed Mr. Leedy. "At last!" he added, giving Mr. Jones a look.

When the applause died down, Mr. Leedy invited everyone to file up onstage to get a good look at the big plants. A line quickly formed and started up the steps.

Mr. Jones grabbed Mr. Leedy's arm and dragged him aside.

"Those plants are alive!" he whispered with a wild look on his face.

"Of course they're alive," replied Mr. Leedy. "Artificial plants were against the rules!"

"But I saw them," said Mr. Jones. "I'm not kidding!"

"We all see them," said Mr. Leedy. "What's your problem?"

Mr. Jones pulled the principal farther into a backstage corner. He put his head close to Mr. Leedy's ear.

"I saw them move," said Mr. Jones. "They grabbed on to things with their vines and rolled themselves around! I told you those plants were trouble last spring. Remember when I said, 'Mark my words. Those plants are trouble'?"

Mr. Leedy shook his head. "You also thought the gym might be haunted," he said, "when you heard burps at night while the science fair was in here!"

He noticed three first graders had edged close and were looking up at them with wide eyes.

"Little pitchers have big ears," he said. "We'll have to discuss this later."

He went back to mingle with the crowd and greet parents. Stanley and Fluffy were proving to be a popular attraction. Michael and Norman were answering questions about the plants.

Mr. Leedy noticed the boys making little twitching motions behind their backs. They seemed to be holding on to some of their plants' vines. He thought it was wonderful that they were so fond of them.

Dad also noticed the twitching motions. He came over to Mr. Leedy. "What time is the truck coming?" he inquired.

"Nine-thirty sharp," said Mr. Leedy. From then on, Dad kept glancing at his watch.

Chapter 14

By nine-fifteen, most of the people had gone home, taking their plants with them. Dad was helping Mr. Jones lower Stanley to the gym floor when the school secretary hurried in.

"The driver just called," she said. "The truck broke down. He was calling from the mobile phone in the tow truck. He thinks the repair will take about an hour."

"Sorry for the delay," said Mr. Leedy. He went to call home to say he would be getting back later than expected.

Mr. Leedy stayed in the office to do some paperwork while they waited.

An hour and a half later, the driver called. The repairs were taking longer than expected. He would be there in another hour or so.

Mr. Leedy came down to the gym to tell them. "Why don't you just go home, and we'll have the plants delivered to you tomorrow," he said.

"We can't leave them here overnight," said Mom.

"But they'll be perfectly safe," said Mr. Leedy.

"We really don't mind waiting another hour or so," said Dad.

"OK," said Mr. Leedy, "but I've got to get home. I'll see if Mr. Jones can stay a little longer. Nobody can be in the building without an official employee on the premises."

Mr. Jones agreed to stay.

As Mr. Leedy was leaving, he said, "There's a coffee maker and soft drink machine in the teachers' lounge. There might be some leftover fruit and doughnuts in the refrigerator there. Use the library, too, if you want something to read."

"We really appreciate this," said Mom.

"I'm just sorry about the truck problem," he said.

"That's OK," said Dad. He told Mom, "If you want to take the boys home, I'll stay."

Norman said, "I don't want to go home! This is fun, being in school late at night when nobody else is here."

Michael agreed. "Let's stay," he said.

"All right," said Mom. "But I'm going home. It's been a long day." Mr. Leedy walked her to her car. Mr. Jones locked the door again after they went out.

Michael got a library book to take back to the gym. Norman found a box of soccer balls in a corner of the stage. He rolled one to Fluffy, who pushed it back to him. Then he started tossing it. Fluffy batted it back.

Soon Fluffy got bored and stopped returning the ball. Norman came down from the stage, threw the ball at the basketball hoop, and missed. Then he looked out into the empty hall. Norman had always wanted to run in the halls, but there was always a grown-up saying, "No running in the halls."

But now no one was looking. Norman could not resist. He took off running. It felt great, pouring on the speed. The whole hall was his! At the end the hall he

89

turned left. He skidded into the turn and almost collided with Dad, who was running toward him. They both stopped.

Dad laughed. "When I was a kid," he said, "I always wanted to run in the halls, but nobody ever let me!" He and Norman started running together back toward the gym. As they passed the door marked TEACHERS' LOUNGE, a voice called out: "No running in the halls!"

They stopped. Mr. Jones stuck his head out and laughed. "Just habit," he said. "Since nobody's here, if you want to run, go ahead. As a matter of fact, I've always wanted to do that myself."

"Join us," said Dad. "We won't tell if you won't."

"That's a deal," replied Mr. Jones. The three of them ran joyfully down the hall and back again.

Norman followed Mr. Jones and Dad into the teachers' lounge. While Mr. Jones made coffee, Dad chuckled over the cartoons and funny signs on the bulletin board.

Norman had never seen this room except for small glimpses when the door was open as he walked by. He bounced on some soft chairs. He sat at the big table and pretended he was a teacher eating lunch.

Dad gave him some coins to get an orange soda from the machine. "Go see if Michael wants something," said Dad. Norman went to the gym.

"Just between us," began Mr. Jones, "there's something wrong with those plants, isn't there?"

"What do you mean?" asked Dad.

Mr. Jones continued, "I knew at the science fair that there was something funny about them. And tonight before I opened the curtains, I saw them grab on to things with their vines and roll themselves along. Then the bigger one lifted a vine and stuck it out between the curtains. That's not normal!''

Dad explained, ''All plants move, but they do it so slowly that you don't notice. Ours just move a little faster. So naturally you'd notice that.''

Norman and Michael came in. ''Can I have an orange soda?'' Michael asked. Dad gave him change.

''I was just explaining to Mr. Jones how our plants move faster than most plants, so that's why he noticed them moving behind the curtains tonight.''

''Oh, yeah,'' said Michael. ''But they're not the only ones that move fast. Did you ever see a Venus's-flytrap? When a bug lands on their sticky parts with the spines sticking out, WHAP! It closes right up!''

''Right!'' added Dad. ''Now, that's what I call moving! Of course, what ours do is pretty unexpected behavior from plants. People hearing about it find it impossible to believe.''

''You said it,'' said Mr. Jones. ''Mr. Leedy didn't believe me.''

Dad noticed both boys were still there. ''Nobody's watching the plants,'' he said.

''Uh-oh,'' said Michael. He ran back to the gym with his can of soda.

''You have to watch them every minute?'' asked Mr. Jones. ''Why is that?''

''We wouldn't want Fluffy to fall off the stage,'' said Dad. Norman took off for the gym, too.

The boys found Stanley had been trying to move around the gym floor. He had pulled over some of the plant display stands, which were too light to hold his weight.

91

Michael thought Stanley might be acting up because he was hungry or upset about not being home now that it was getting late.

Sitting down on the floor, Michael took off his shoes and socks. Stanley snatched the socks from his hands and sucked up both at the same time with a loud *schlurrp!*

"Don't gobble," scolded Michael. "Where are your manners?" Michael took a gulp of his orange soda and burped.

"Where are my manners?" he asked himself.

Norman came in and bounded up onstage. Fluffy was beginning to move around, so Norman decided to calm him down by singing.

Mr. Jones ran in to see what the horrible noise was. He arrived just as Stanley, digesting his meal, gave two hearty burps.

"That's it!" yelled Mr. Jones. "That's what I heard that night at the science fair!"

Michael held up his soda can. "Excuse me," he said. "This always happens when I drink carbonated stuff. It's so embarrassing to burp that big."

Mr. Jones looked at him suspiciously. "Who knocked over these stands?" he asked.

Michael said, "They were that way when I came back from the teachers' lounge."

Norman decided to help. He suggested, "Maybe there was a little earthquake."

Dad strolled in. "I called the repair place," he said. "The truck left ten minutes ago. They should be here pretty soon."

"Good," said Mr. Jones. "I'll go close up the unlocked rooms so I can go home."

Fortunately, he had not noticed Fluffy waving vines up on the stage, where the lights were turned off.

"Can you get that plant settled down before the truck comes?" asked Dad.

Michael told Norman, "Just don't sing. Maybe if we turned the stage lights on, Fluffy would think it was daytime and slow down."

"I'll do it!" said Norman. He disappeared off to the side. In the quiet gym, Michael heard him flipping the switches—thunk, thunk, thunk. One bright light after another flooded the stage. Fluffy calmed down.

Norman poked his head out from the side. "It's the Norman and Fluffy Show!" he proclaimed.

"Can we close the curtains?" Michael asked Dad crossly.

But Norman had accidentally turned on the microphone switch, too. Fluffy, who was next to the mike, gave a burp that boomed out over the gym, echoed off the walls and ceiling, and could be heard all the way down the hall.

Mr. Jones hurried in. "That's it! That's the ghost! Where is it?"

Dad said calmly, "It's just one of the plants making a little noise."

"I knew it!" said Mr. Jones. "It *had* to be those weird plants!"

Michael asked Norman, "Did you give Fluffy a sock?"

"Yeah," he answered. "Mom gave it to me in case of emergency."

When the truck driver entered the gym a few minutes later, he was startled to hear a very loud noise that sounded like "Ex" boom from the microphone. But he saw that no one was standing near the mike or the large plant next to it.

"What was that!" exclaimed the driver.

Mr. Jones replied, "Never mind. You wouldn't believe it anyway."

They loaded the plants into the truck and headed home.

Chapter 15

The next morning the boys were too tired to put the plants through their house-chore practice.

"But I think we're ready," said Michael. "We can't wait much longer."

They got their chance that evening. After dinner, the family went shopping together. When they carried the groceries into the kitchen, Mom mentioned that she and Dad were going down the street for a few minutes to take a present to the Johnsons for their new baby.

"Do you want to come along and see the baby?" she asked the boys.

"Nope," said Michael. This was the perfect opportunity. He poked Norman in the ribs to get his attention. "Norman and I can put the groceries away," he told Mom.

"Huh?" said Norman, wondering why his brother was volunteering them both to do this. Michael poked him again. It dawned on him that he should go along with this idea. "We'll do it. Yeah," he said.

"You're offering?" said Mom, looking amazed. "Well, all right. We won't be gone long."

When they heard the front door close, Michael said, "This is our big chance. We can get set up while they're out, and have the plants already doing chores when they get back." They ran to get Stanley and Fluffy from their room.

Norman exclaimed, "Are they ever going to be surprised!"

In the yard Norman made sure Fluffy kept the hose aimed at the flowers. He adjusted the nozzle to get a good wide spray on the impatiens. They needed more water than the geraniums and marigolds. If they didn't get enough, they got droopy. Norman wanted to be sure Fluffy gave them a good soaking. He was delighted to see how steady Fluffy was holding the hose.

In the kitchen Michael guided Stanley through the motions of picking up a package or can from a grocery bag and lifting it over to the cupboard. There Michael guided Stanley's vine to the right place and told him to let go. He handled the glass bottles and jars himself. He didn't want to take a chance on Stanley dropping anything breakable.

As Michael put a jar of pickles on a shelf, Stanley picked up a half-gallon carton of orange juice. It was heavy, so he used three vines. He must have sensed what was in it, because he began shaking it. The sloshing noise made Michael turn around.

"No," he said. "Let me have that."

But Stanley didn't hand over the carton. He squeezed it with the full force of three vines. It popped apart. The air was filled with flying juice.

Michael untangled what was left of the carton from Stanley's vines. With juice dripping off the end of his nose, he went to the sink to get paper towels. He opened the window over the sink and yelled to Norman, "Get in here quick!"

Behind his back, Stanley was feeling around in the grocery bag for another carton.

"Why?" asked Norman, stalling to let Michael know he wouldn't be bossed.

"Hurry!" called Michael. "It's a cleanup emergency!"

Norman told Fluffy, "Don't move." He sprinted in the back door. As he came in, Michael turned back toward Stanley just as the plant burst a second carton. More flying juice splattered all over.

The roll of paper towels Michael was holding became a soggy, unrollable mess. Norman opened a drawer to get out cloth towels to start wiping up. Michael put his head under the faucet to rinse the juice off his hair.

Stanley, who was having a great time, hoisted another carton from another grocery bag and popped it. This time milk spewed everywhere. The kitchen looked as if it had been redecorated by a very messy painter.

But Stanley didn't seem pleased about getting drenched in milk. Apparently he had been expecting more juice. He shook himself like a wet dog, hurling liquid everywhere, including the ceiling. There drops hung and began falling—plop, plop, plop.

Stanley decided to try again. Before Michael could stop him, he plucked a bag of flour from another bag. He raised it high, out of the boys' reach, and started shaking it. With a loud pop, the paper package burst. Flour sifted gently down all over.

When the white stuff settled, Stanley looked like a ghost plant. Michael and Norman looked like junior versions of the Abominable Snowman.

Norman wiped the goo off his glasses. He asked, "Does juice and milk and flour make paste like water and flour?" Plop, plop went more drops from the ceiling.

Michael, scraping goo off his shirt, replied, "Yeah, I think we just discovered a new recipe for paste. Or possibly, when it dries, cement." He surveyed the mess. "You're the cleaning expert," he told Norman. "Where do we start?"

"I don't know," answered Norman. "This is too much. I give up."

Michael said, "Come on, we can do it. We have to hurry. They'll be home soon."

He kept moving around, trying to dodge drops from the ceiling. Norman handed him a bunch of towels. But everywhere they wiped, more drops plopped.

Michael said, "We have to get the stepladder and wipe the ceiling first. Stanley can help."

But he heard the front door open.

"We're home," called Dad.

Michael did the only thing he could think of in a panic. He pushed the kitchen door shut and turned out the lights.

Norman whispered, "We can't keep them out of here."

"I know," Michael whispered back. "I'm trying to think of something."

"Boys!" called Mom. "Where are you?" They heard her go down the hall to their room.

"They're not in there!" she told Dad. "And the plants are gone, too! I shudder to think what the logical explanation is for this."

Michael whispered, "Tiptoe to the back door. Maybe

we can escape and come in the front door like we weren't here.''

But they heard Dad on the other side of the kitchen door, saying, ''Where could they be?''

It was too late to run. The door slowly opened. Dad took one step into the dark kitchen and called, ''They're not in here either!''

In the silence, Michael heard plop, plop, plop.

Dad said, ''That's odd. It feels like I'm getting rained on.'' He turned on the light.

''What!'' yelled Dad at the sight. ''What have you done to this kitchen?''

Norman bolted for the back door. Michael grabbed him by his gooey shirt and hung on to him.

Mom walked in and said, ''Oh, no!'' She walked around to inspect the mess. To defend her hair from plopping drops, she put a big metal mixing bowl upside down on her head. The drops hitting her armored hat went plink, plink, plink.

Dad put a roasting pan upside down on his head. The drops hitting that went pong, pong, pong.

Michael was already such a soggy mess that nothing he could put on would be of any use. But Norman, desperate to distract Mom and Dad from whatever punishment they were sure to unleash, grabbed an umbrella from the broom closet. He started sliding around the wet floor, dancing and bellowing the song ''Singin' in the Rain.'' He had seen Gene Kelly do this in a movie on TV.

Michael thought Norman deserved a lot of credit for doing his best in the face of disaster. He told him, ''Maybe you should change the words to 'Singin' in the Juice.' '' Norman took him up on that suggestion. As he sang, mostly off-key, Stanley waved his white vines to the music, giving off little puffs of flour into the air as he moved.

When Norman finished, there was silence except for plop, plink, pong, plink, pong, plop.

Dad said, "First, you're going to clean this up, even if it takes all night. Then, until your mother and I figure out what the penalty will be for this monumental mess, you're grounded for the rest of your lives. That includes Stanley until he leaves town." He paused. "Wait a minute. Where's Fluffy?"

As if in answer to his question, through the open window over the sink came a torrential spray of water from the hose outside.

After the boys explained what they had been trying to do, Mom and Dad were not as mad.

Mom said, "I understand how much you want to keep your plants. You certainly have worked hard to teach them to help around the house. But look how it turned out. Disaster! They'll be much better off in a botanical garden."

"But they didn't mean to make a mess," pointed out Michael.

Dad said, "We all know they don't mean to cause trouble, but that's what keeps happening."

Michael rolled Stanley outside. He washed the flour, juice, and milk off him with the hose and some towels.

Norman took Fluffy inside. He showed his parents how Fluffy could be helpful by giving him a damp dishcloth and having him wipe the ceiling. Norman got up on the stepladder to wipe the spots that Fluffy missed.

Mom and Dad were impressed, but this didn't change their minds. But Norman and Michael looked so down-hearted that their parents took pity on them.

"We'll help you clean up," said Dad, "because if we don't, it probably really will take all night."

As they worked, Dad pointed out, "A botanical garden will be perfect for Stanley and Fluffy. They'll be well cared for by experts. They'll have a warm climate all year—and lots of sunlight through the glass walls and roof."

Norman looked glum.

"And the roof there must be forty feet high," Dad continued. "They can grow as tall as they want. If they stayed here, they'd soon be bumping into the ceiling. That would be terrible for them."

Michael pictured Stanley and Fluffy bending over to grow sideways along the ceiling in their room, back down the opposite wall, and across the floor. That would be uncomfortable.

He suggested, "We can cut two holes in the ceiling so they can grow through it into the attic."

Dad said, "But their tops would be in the dark all the time."

Michael said, "We could put special grow lights up there."

Norman said, "Let's rip off the roof and make a big skylight!"

Dad put an arm around each boy and pulled them close. "Sons, I know this is hard for you, but the plants *have* to go live in a botanical garden. We'll go and visit them. You'll see. It'll be for the best."

"No," cried Norman. "It'll be for the worst. Fluffy would miss me something awful. Nobody can take care of him like me!'' He pulled away from Dad angrily. ''If Fluffy goes, I'm going. I'll go live in the botanical garden, too.'' He ran out of the room.

Chapter 16

Michael finally accepted the fact that Stanley had to go. He had run out of ideas. Maybe it would be better for botanists to take care of Stanley and Fluffy, after all.

Now that they had only a few days left to be together, Michael spent as much time as he could with his plant. He mostly just sat quietly beside Stanley and occasionally talked to him.

"I'm really going to miss you," he said. "But I'll come and visit. We'll always be friends. And I'll never forget you."

But Norman was frantic. He started having temper tantrums. He kicked furniture and threw things. He was grumpy most of the time that he wasn't talking or singing to Fluffy. He rolled his plant along everywhere he went in the house, even the bathroom. During every meal, Fluffy stood beside him at the table.

The few times he neglected to take Fluffy with him, the plant grabbed furniture and doorknobs and pulled himself along to follow Norman. Mom had to barricade the front door one morning to keep Fluffy from flinging himself out of the house to follow Norman to school.

She kept calm by keeping up her daily countdown. Eight more days. Seven more days. Six more days. Then they were down to five.

The fifth-to-the-last day was a Wednesday. Michael dawdled in the school library after school because he stopped in to check out a book and found six more he wanted to borrow. He also stopped to talk to Brad on the way home, so he arrived later than usual.

Because Michael's arms were full of books, he used his elbow to ring the door bell. But Norman did not come.

Grumbling to himself, Michael put his things down, sorted through his pockets to find his key, and unlocked the door. He picked up his books, kicked the door shut, and dumped the books on the nearest chair.

"Where are you?" he yelled. There was no answer. Norman wasn't in the kitchen, but there was a clue on the table that he had been there. A plate of raisin cookies was exactly half-empty. Norman had eaten his share. Michael went to look in their room.

Fluffy was gone. Michael went to look in the backyard. No Norman. No Fluffy. He must have taken the plant over to Bob's, even though they weren't allowed to take the plants anywhere. So Norman was planning to be back before Mom got home. Michael decided he wouldn't tell on Norman. He understood how he felt. It was his last chance to go somewhere with his plant.

Michael poured a glass of milk and sat down to eat his share of the cookies. Glancing around, he noticed six baked beans on the floor. Norman must have been making a baked-bean sandwich. But why would he do that when he had cookies? And why didn't he clean up the scattered beans? That wasn't like him, unless he was upset for some reason. Very odd, Michael thought. Of course, Norman had been upset for a long time about losing Fluffy.

Michael pulled Mom's usual Wednesday note from under the plate. "Back by 5:30," it said. "Michael, your turn to set the table. Both start your homework. No arguing. Love, Mom."

He noticed another piece of paper sticking out from under the plate. It was a note printed by Norman, who did not worry about spelling when he was in a hurry: "Der Mom and Dad, Im going away with Fluffy becus you wont let me keep him. I hate you. Love, Norman. P.S. Michael I want to save Stanly to but to plnts is to hevy to pul with my bik."

Michael panicked. He tried to calm down and think of what to do. He ran out the front door and looked both ways. He looked in the garage in case Norman was just bluffing and hiding out there. Since he hadn't passed Norman and Fluffy on the way home from the library, they must have gone in another direction. But which one?

He tried to figure out how big a head start Norman had. From the time they usually got home from school, it had been thirty or forty minutes. With time out for eating cookies, making a baked-bean sandwich, tying Fluffy to the bike with a rope, and writing the note, Michael thought, Norman had probably been gone about fifteen or twenty minutes.

If he jumped on his bike and pedaled like crazy, maybe he could catch up with Norman and bring him back. But that wouldn't work if Michael picked the wrong direction. Too bad there wasn't a trail of baked beans to follow. Norman must have wrapped up the sandwich.

But he couldn't just stand there in a panic doing nothing. Every minute that he stood here, Norman was getting farther and farther away.

Then he realized that Bob's house was probably where Norman would go. He called. Bob was home, but Norman wasn't there. Michael asked Bob to look around the neighborhood.

The doorbell rang. Michael leaped to answer it. Maybe Norman had come home and didn't have his key. He yanked the door open before looking out to see who was there. It was Mrs. Smith. "I saw you come home," she said, "and I know your mother is at work on Wednesday afternoons. I'm worried about Norman. Did he come back yet?"

"He ran away," Michael blurted out. "He left a note."

Mrs. Smith said, "That explains it. He passed my yard, pulling his plant with his bike, about twenty minutes ago. When I asked him where he was going, he said they were going for a long, long ride. He didn't stop to talk. That isn't like him. He just kept going. And he looked upset."

Michael said, "I'll go after him, now that I know which way to go."

"Have you called your parents?" asked Mrs. Smith.

"No, but—"

"Let's do that first," she said. "Then I'll go after him in my car. That'll be faster. You stay here in case he calls home."

Michael called Dad at work. Dad said he'd call Mom

and come right home. He told Michael to check Norman's things to see what he was wearing and what he might have taken along.

"Why?" asked Michael.

"So we'll have a good description in case we don't find him right away and have to call the police."

Michael said, "Maybe if he didn't take his duffel bag, he's not going to stay away long."

"And if he calls, or comes home before we get there," said Dad, "tell him we love him and we're not going to be mad at him. We just want him home."

Mrs. Smith got on the phone to tell Dad she was setting out to look for Norman right away. Then she hurried off.

Michael found that Norman's duffel bag was gone. He tried to remember what Norman was wearing that morning when they left for school. He got a piece of paper and wrote down: "Blue duffel bag. Blue and green jacket." He started looking through Norman's bureau drawers, but he couldn't tell if anything was missing until he got to the sock drawer. It was empty. Norman had taken more than a week's worth of clean socks for Fluffy. With a sinking feeling, Michael added to the list: "Lots of socks, mostly fudge ripple."

The ring of the doorbell made him jump. This time it was Bob, looking worried.

"Did he come home yet?" asked Bob.

"No," said Michael. "Mrs. Smith saw him riding away on his bike, pulling Fluffy. She went to look for him in her car. My Mom and Dad are on their way home."

Bob said, "I looked all over for him, but I couldn't find him."

Michael asked, "Did he say anything to you about running away?"

"Nope. But this morning on the way to school he said he was going to save Fluffy from going to that garden, but he didn't know how. Where could he be? Why didn't he run away to my house? I'm his best friend. He could stay with me."

Michael said, "That would have been the smart thing for him to do."

Bob said, "I'm really worried. What if he never comes back?"

"We'll find him," said Michael, to reassure Bob and himself.

"I got so mad last week that I wanted to run away," said Bob. "But I decided not to. We were having meat loaf and mashed potatoes for dinner."

They sat in silence for a few moments. Then Bob said, "If I ever run away, can I come here and stay?"

"Sure," said Michael.

They heard a car pull into the drive, and two car doors slam. Mom and Dad burst into the house.

"Any news?" said Mom, looking frantic.

"Not yet," replied Michael. "I started a list of what he took. Wait a minute. I thought of one more thing." He wrote down: "Baked-bean sandwich."

Mom looked around the kitchen to see what other food he might have taken. Some little cans of juice were missing, and a couple of bananas.

"This is terrible," said Mom. "He's not planning to be home for dinner. I'm so worried!"

"Me, too," said Bob.

Dad patted Bob's shoulder. "We're all worried," he said, "but we'll find him."

Michael said, "I should have been here. I was late getting home. I could have stopped him."

"It's not your fault," said Dad, hugging him. He put an arm out for Mom. She came over to be hugged, too. So did Bob. Mom and Dad had tears in their eyes. Then Dad blew his nose and said, "Okay, let's figure out what to do."

Just then Mrs. Smith called. She hadn't found Norman, but she was going to keep looking. Dad took notes about what area she had searched and where she was going to look next. He got a city map from the car and marked the part she was covering.

"I'll take the car and do this area," he said, circling part of the map. I'll call in every fifteen minutes or so. Mrs. Smith will call in, too. Michael, you cover this area on your bike. You might be able to see things we can't see from a car on the road." Dad explained where he should go and gave him change for pay phones.

"Hurry," said Mom. "It'll be getting dark in a couple of hours."

Michael grabbed his jacket and tucked a flashlight in his pocket in case he had to keep looking after dark. As he set off, he noticed a chill in the air.

Where could Norman have disappeared to?

Chapter 17

About four miles from home, Norman was getting tired from pedaling with Fluffy's weight behind the bike.

He had not planned to run away. When he got home that afternoon, he looked at Fluffy and thought about how, in only four days, his plant would be taken away. It wasn't fair. Dad and Mom were being so mean. Anger swept over him. On the spur of the moment, he thought, if I run away with Fluffy, nobody can take him away from me. There was nobody there to stop him.

Michael would probably be home any minute, so he had to hurry. He packed, wrote the note, and was speeding away with Fluffy in tow within five minutes.

As he pedaled away, he thought, "They'll be really sorry when they find out I'm gone!"

When Mrs. Smith asked him where he was going, he almost told her he was running away. But he didn't, even though he half hoped she would talk him out of it. He was so angry, he just wanted to keep going.

As he passed Bob's house, he slowed up, hoping Bob

would see him and run out and ask where he was going. But Bob didn't come out. Norman kept pedaling.

The street slanted slightly uphill, so pulling Fluffy was not easy. As his anger wore off, Norman realized that he had no idea where he was going. He had been so upset that he hadn't given that any thought. He just wanted to get away and save Fluffy. After a while there were more and more cars on the road. He saw the park sign, so he turned off there and stopped under a big tree to eat his baked-bean sandwich. When he sat down, the ground was wet, so he had to stand up to eat.

He told Fluffy, "Don't worry, I brought plenty of socks for you to eat." Fluffy put a vine around Norman's shoulder.

Norman had no idea what to do next. He was still hungry, so he ate a banana and dropped the peel on the ground. Norman never littered, but now he didn't care. He drank a can of juice and dropped the empty can next to the plastic sandwich bag and the banana peel.

He leaned against Fluffy for comfort. "I don't know where we're going," he told the plant. "I don't know what to do."

It was a beautiful fall afternoon, but it was getting chilly. Some trees were still green, but many were turning gold, orange, red, and brown. Joggers and bicyclists kept coming by. Most of them glanced at Norman as they passed. What they saw was a boy standing under a big tree and beside a large plant, which from a distance appeared to be growing there. On the handlebar of the bike propped against the tree hung a small duffel bag of the kind many people carry their gym clothes in. So no one noticed that Norman was running away.

But all those people looking at him made Norman nervous. What if somebody stopped and asked him what he was doing there? Or what if some weirdo tried to kidnap him? He looked into the woods, where colored leaves carpeted the ground and a path led deeper into the trees. An arrow-shaped sign that said LOOKOUT POINT pointed to the path. He decided to go that way, away from the road.

The going was slow. The beaten dirt path had many muddy places. It was a bumpy ride for Fluffy. His skateboard wheels became clogged with mud and wet leaves. He tipped over a couple of times.

Norman got all muddy using his fingers to scrape the junk off Fluffy's wheels. Finally, after many such stops, they emerged from the woods. Ahead was an asphalt road and parking places with yellow stripes. Beyond that was a sign that said LOOKOUT POINT on a thick brown wooden railing, and a vast view of the sky with puffy white clouds.

Norman realized this place must be sort of high up. Pulling up to the railing, which was the height of his shoulders, he looked over. He was on top of a cliff ledge that sloped down on the other side of the railing. Spread out below him were thick green treetops. Beyond those he saw little houses and buildings and streets where tiny cars and trucks and buses ran like small bugs.

Norman wondered if he could camp out in the park. But he wasn't prepared for that. He didn't even have a blanket. And a cold night would surely make Fluffy sick.

Norman had no idea where to go, but he couldn't

turn around and go back home. He hoped that by now they would be looking for him.

Norman had lost track of time. He looked at his Mickey Mouse watch and found it was five-fifteen. Then he recalled that Mom's note said she would be home at five-thirty. So maybe she didn't even know yet. But if Michael was home by now, surely he would have called Mom and Dad so they could all start looking. But what if Michael hadn't come home yet? That meant nobody was looking for him yet. Norman's heart sank. They had to come after him. They had to!

But then terrible thoughts began going through his head. He wondered, what if Michael wants to have our room all to himself? What if he's glad that I ran away? What if he tore up my note so Mom and Dad won't know what happened to me? What if Mom and Dad read my note, but won't come looking to teach me a lesson?

Tears spilled from his eyes. He hadn't packed tissues, so he wiped his eyes and nose on his jacket sleeve. Fluffy patted him on the head and stroked his hair. Norman threw his arms around Fluffy, and Fluffy threw his vines around Norman. Soon Norman was feeling better.

He pictured Mom being horrified when she read his note at five-thirty. ''My precious baby!'' she would cry, because that's what she used to call him when he was little. She hadn't called him that lately because he didn't like to be called a baby. She would say, ''We have to find him and let him keep his plant!'' Dad would come home and call the police. They would all run out of the house looking for him. Michael would lead the police on his bicycle. Maybe the police would put out an APB and search parties. That would be good, because that way he would get found a lot faster and in time for dinner.

Norman told Fluffy, "We have to go back closer to home so they can find us, but we better wait till five-thirty."

Now that he had decided how to get found, he felt somewhat cheered up. His watch said five-twenty. Time was going really slow. He decided to wait till five-thirty-five to give Mom time to get in the house, go in the kitchen, and read the note, in case Michael hadn't already found it.

He started humming and then broke into singing "Oh, Susanna," hitting a few wrong notes as usual. Fluffy waved a vine in time to the music and rustled his leaves happily. After Norman sang the song three times, he lost interest and turned back to the railing to enjoy the view again.

Nearby, he noticed, on the other side of the railing, was a straggly little tree growing up over the edge of the cliff. He recognized the fan-shaped leaves. It was a ginkgo. If he had one of those leaves, he could get Michael to give him something he wanted in exchange for it. The nearest leaves were just out of his reach, so he ducked under the railing. As he stepped near the edge, he cautiously held on to the railing with one hand and reached as far as he could with the other. But no matter how hard he stretched, the leaves were still about six inches from his fingertips.

So Norman let go of the railing just for a moment, balanced himself carefully, and took one step closer.

As he snapped the leaf off, the soil and flaked rock beneath him crumbled. His feet began sliding. Norman

114

twisted his body around to grab the railing, but his feet went out from under him and he landed on his stomach. With his fingers digging into the crumbling surface, the harder he tried to get a foothold, the more dirt and rock fell away.

"Fluffy!" cried Norman. "Help! Help!" He slid a little farther. Fluffy just stood there on the other side of the railing, as if he were puzzled about what Norman meant.

Norman's fingers started sliding, making claw marks in the dirt. "Grab, Fluffy, grab!" he shrieked.

With a couple of vines, Fluffy firmly grabbed the railing.

"No, me!" shouted Norman. "Fluffy, grab me!" The giant plant leaned against the railing and whirled all his other vines in all directions except down, where Norman was.

"Grab down here!" Norman called. Fluffy kept whirling in confusion. He had never grabbed below ground level, and he was having trouble getting the idea.

Frantically Norman grabbed at a clump of weeds he had slid within reach of, but it pulled loose in his hand. Then, in spite of his total panic, it dawned on him that he should keep up a steady sound for Fluffy to follow.

He was scared out of his mind, but he began singing one of his and Fluffy's favorite songs. "Camptown ladies sing this song," he howled slightly off-key. "Doo-dah, doo-dah." His voice was shaking, but he kept going.

Fluffy stopped whirling and started reaching around lower. He was almost there.

Norman noticed he was near the bottom of the thin trunk of the ginkgo tree. Holding on to that would keep

115

him from sliding anymore. Fluffy would reach him in a second.

"Camptown racetrack's five miles long," he sang bravely. "Oh, doo-dah day!" When his right hand closed around the tree, its shallow roots ripped free. He let go, and the tree fell away. He tried not to think about how far down it was falling.

He slid a little more. To his horror, he felt his feet lose touch with the cliff and dangle in midair. But the next moment he stopped falling with a jolt as strong vines wrapped his feet and middle. Fluffy held on with all the strength he could muster.

Norman called, "Thanks, Fluffy, I love you."

Now that he was securely cradled in Fluffy's vines, he tried to scramble back up, but he could not. "Pull up, Fluffy, pull," he instructed.

Fluffy tried, but one vine broke with a snap. "Stop!" called Norman. "Just hold on!" The plant held on.

Norman was stuck, but at least he was safe for as long as Fluffy could hold him.

After he calmed down a little, he looked at his watch: 5:37. They must be looking for him by now. He hoped somebody would come soon. He and Fluffy could use a whole search party to get them out of this.

To keep himself and Fluffy encouraged while they waited, he sang a few "doo-dahs" from time to time. Every few minutes, he also yelled "Help!" in case anyone could hear him.

Chapter 18

Michael set off in the direction Mrs. Smith said Norman had been heading. Since she had already driven along this road, he kept turning off down side streets and then back to the main one. Every couple of blocks, he stopped and yelled Norman's name.

Long before he got near the park, the evening rush-hour traffic was getting heavy. He didn't think Norman would have stayed on the road with so many cars, especially when he was towing Fluffy. The quiet park roads would be safer. Michael turned in to the park at the first entrance road he came to.

He got off his bike and pushed it along, so he could look closely at the muddy ground beside the road. Then he saw what looked like skateboard tracks, and slowed down. He almost missed where they turned away from the road. The grassy places didn't show any traces of tracks, but every so often there were more muddy patches. Marks in the mud led him to a large tree. Under it he found a plastic sandwich bag, a banana peel, and an empty juice can like the kind Norman had taken.

But this junk couldn't be Norman's. He would have

put the peel and can in the bag and carried it until he found a trash container.

Then Michael looked more closely at the plastic bag. In it were four more baked beans the same size and shade of brown as the ones that had fallen out of Norman's sandwich in the kitchen. He had been here!

Quickly inspecting the ground all around, Michael found another wheel track at the beginning of the trail marked Lookout Point. He got back on his bike and rode into the woods. Crisp leaves crunched under his wheels. His front wheel sank into a mud patch, throwing him over. As he got up, he saw a green leaf lying atop the yellow, red, and brown leaves of the forest. It was one of Fluffy's. The plant must have tipped over here.

"Norman!" he yelled. There was no answer. He hurried on. Thinking he heard something, he stopped to listen. But it was far-off. It might be a voice. He bounced on along the path, slipping and sliding. He stopped again to listen. This time he recognized the sound. It was a faint, familiar voice singing, "Oh, Susanna."

Michael felt relieved and annoyed at the same time. Everybody was worried sick, and here Norman was just hanging around the park singing—and probably scaring the squirrels and birds with the noise.

Racing on, Michael burst out of the woods. Across the parking spaces, he saw Fluffy braced against a thick wooden railing and leaning over it, with all his vines reaching down. They were stretched taut.

Michael dropped his bike and ran to the railing. Norman was hanging around the park, but not the way Michael expected. His body was tightly cradled in Fluffy's vines. His feet were in midair.

118

"Help!" said Norman. "Fluffy's got me, but he can't pull me up!"

Michael said, "I'll pull on Fluffy."

"No!" said Norman. "His vines might break. One already did."

Michael lay down on the ground and tried to reach his brother. He needed to hang on to the posts or crossbar of the railing to keep himself from sliding off the cliff, but he couldn't reach Norman that way.

"Let me think a minute," he said. "Can Fluffy hold you a little longer while I go find help?"

"No, he's been holding me a long time. He looks tired. I'm really scared."

Michael saw the plant was still tied to Norman's bike with the tow rope. The knot wouldn't come apart fast enough, so he cut the rope, quickly sawing it with his pocketknife. He made a big loop with that end, and a square knot. He pulled on it hard to make sure it wouldn't slip. Then he lowered the loop to Norman.

"Hang on with both hands," he said. He lined up Norman's bike, still tied to the other end of the rope. Then he got on and pressed the pedals with all his might. The bike inched along, dragging Norman up and just over the edge.

Norman's feet were back on ground. "I'm up!" he shouted. Michael dragged him a little farther to make sure. Then he dropped the bike and went to help him. But he couldn't pull him under the railing, because Fluffy's vines hanging over the railing were still wrapped tightly around him.

"Tell Fluffy he can let go now," said Michael. With Norman talking and singing to him, Fluffy slowly began to relax his grip. He looked exhausted and could hardly

119

move his vines. So Michael gently untangled them from Norman.

Norman looked almost as bad as Fluffy. His jacket and face were smeared with dirt. His hair stood up in little tufts pointing in all directions. Dirt encrusted his fingernails. Dirt was embedded in his shoelaces. When he stood up, he staggered a little until he got his balance.

The first thing he did was hug Fluffy. Then he threw his arms around Michael.

"Are you OK?" asked Michael, patting him on the back.

"Yeah," replied Norman, snuffling. "I am now."

Michael said, "We have to find a phone and call home. Dad and Mrs. Smith are out looking for you, too."

"What about Mom?" asked Norman.

"She's frantic, too. She's home waiting for you or anybody who finds you to call. Whatever made you think running away was a good idea?"

"I didn't think," replied Norman. "I just wanted to save Fluffy."

"But Fluffy saved you," said Michael.

"Are Mom and Dad going to be mad at me?" asked Norman.

"Dad said they wouldn't. They'll just be glad to get you back. They were worried sick."

"Were you worried?" asked Norman.

"Yeah, me, too. Come on. Let's go home."

They retied the tow rope around Fluffy and tucked his vines carefully around him so they wouldn't drag. He was still too tired to lift them. They took the Lookout Point road out of the park to the main road.

Halfway home they saw a public phone.

"I found him," Michael told Mom. "He was in the park. He's OK. We're on the way home."

Mom insisted on talking to Norman to be sure he was all right. "Hurry home," she said.

She and Mrs. Smith and Bob were waiting on the curb when the boys and Fluffy rode down the street. Mom hugged Norman so hard, he couldn't breathe. Then she hugged Michael just as hard.

Mrs. Smith went on home, saying she wanted to hear all about it later. Bob followed them into the house.

Michael was just explaining how he found Norman's tracks when they heard the car zoom into the drive. Dad rushed in and hugged Norman breathless again.

"Where have you been?" Dad asked. But Norman couldn't reply immediately because all the air had been squashed out of him again.

"He was in the park," said Mom.

"What were you doing in the park?" asked Dad, letting go.

Norman sucked in some air and replied, "I was hanging off a cliff."

This news had a dramatic effect on Mom, Dad, and Bob. They looked aghast.

"But Fluffy saved me," Norman continued. "He held on to me over the edge for the longest time until Michael came. So I didn't fall off."

"It's true," said Michael. "Fluffy was a hero!"

Everyone turned to look at Fluffy. He still looked awful. He was bent over. His leaves were limp and bedraggled. He even seemed a paler shade of green than usual.

Michael said, "He saved Norman's life. He should get a big reward."

121

"Like what?" asked Bob.

"We should give him a good home forever with the person who cares about him more than anybody else ever could—Norman!"

"Yeah," said Norman.

"That's right," said Bob.

This suggestion was greeted with silence from Mom and Dad.

Then Norman piped up, "Michael helped save me, too. Fluffy couldn't drag me up. Michael did it, so he should get a big reward, too."

"Like what?" chimed in Bob. He couldn't have been a better stooge if they'd rehearsed him.

"Stanley," said Norman. "He should get to keep Stanley."

"That's right," said Bob, nodding.

"Bob," said Mom, "isn't it about time for dinner at your house?"

Norman asked, "Can he stay for dinner?"

"Tomorrow," replied Mom. "Bob, ask your mother if you can have dinner with us then."

"OK," said Bob. He turned to Norman. "If you run away again, you should stay at my house. And if I run away, I'll stay at your house."

"OK," said Norman. "But I'm not running away ever again. It was terrible!"

"Cool," said Bob. He dashed out the door.

Norman and Michael just stood around, waiting for Dad and Mom to say something about rewards for saving Norman.

But Dad only said, "What are we having for dinner?"

"Before that," said Mom, "we better do first aid on Fluffy." Michael thought that was a good sign.

They gathered around to take care of the plant. Norman watered him, because he was all dried out from his efforts. Mom gently wiped the dust and mud smears from his leaves. Michael slowly dripped orange juice into his ice-cream-cone-shaped leaves. Dad cut a fudge ripple sock into small pieces to make it easier to eat. Norman coaxed Fluffy to eat by putting the tiny pieces into a rolled-up leaf. Fluffy made small, feeble *schlurp* sounds.

Dad said, "OK, now what are we having for dinner?"

"I have no idea," said Mom. "Somebody suggest something."

Michael said, "Norman and I can make dinner."

"No," said Mom, "we've been through enough uproars already today."

"No, really," said Michael. "We can do it. We'll surprise you," he said. "Go in the living room and wait."

Mom and Dad wanted to discuss the plant situation in private anyway, so they did as Michael suggested.

Michael and Norman argued in whispers about what to have for dinner. They decided to compromise. Michael called a pizza delivery place, and Norman started getting out the bread.

Norman said, "Go listen to what they're saying."

"You go," said Michael. "They won't get mad at you if they catch you listening because you almost fell off a cliff."

But Dad and Mom were arguing in such quiet whispers that he could not make out what they were saying.

Twenty minutes later, Dad and Mom were surprised when the doorbell rang. Michael ran to answer it. A delivery man handed over a large pizza. Michael paid for it with his own money.

"Dinner's ready," he said, and led the way to the dining room. The table was nicely set with four chairs and six plates. Fluffy, who was looking better now, and Stanley stood at two of the places. On the plates for Mom, Dad, Michael, and Norman were baked-bean sandwiches. On Fluffy and Stanley's plates were fudge ripple socks. The ones for Stanley, of course, which Michael had just taken off, didn't smell too good. But the delicious smell of hot pizza was so overwhelming that nobody seemed to mind.

Michael opened the pizza box and put it in the middle of the table.

"Yum, yum," said Mom, taking a piece.

"I made the sandwiches," said Norman. "It's my new recipe so the beans don't fall out when you eat. I glued them to the bread with margarine and big blobs of catsup."

"Very creative," said Dad.

"Very neat," said Norman. "No more beans on the floor."

"Very tasty," said Mom, trying her sandwich.

Michael passed a dish of carrots and celery he had washed off but not sliced. This led to a lot of loud crunching. For the moment, nobody was talking, just eating. He wondered if he should ask again about keeping the plants, or wait. If they had made up their minds, surely they would say something. But what else could he do to convince them to say yes?

Finally Mom said to Dad, "Do you want to tell them, or shall I?"

Chapter 19

Dad asked Mom, "Are you sure about this decision? You're not going to change your mind?"

"No," she said firmly. "I'm sure."

Michael was afraid the plants were doomed to be sent away. He could see from the expression on Norman's face that he thought so, too.

"This has been a hard decision to make," said Mom solemnly, "but we've decided that we can't get rid of a plant that saved our precious baby. We owe it to Fluffy to keep him."

Norman leaped from his chair and did a little dance of joy around the room, yelling, "Yay! Yay!" Then he hugged Mom and Dad and Fluffy. Fluffy hugged Norman with half his vines and hugged Mom with the other half.

Michael took a deep breath and asked, "What about Stanley?"

"We decided that it wouldn't be fair," said Dad, "to keep one plant and not the other. And you deserve to have something that means so much to you."

Another round of hugging followed.

"It isn't going to be easy," said Mom, "to cope with these plants. But we're willing to work it out. I don't know what we'll do when they get too big for your room."

Michael said, "We should start saving up now for a greenhouse."

Dad agreed, "Maybe we could get a home-improvement loan from a bank. But what if they outgrow the greenhouse?"

Michael explained, "There are home greenhouses where you can grow plants fifteen or twenty feet tall. Or bigger. I've seen pictures of them in books."

Norman asked, "Can I move my bed out in the greenhouse with Fluffy?"

"Wait a minute," said Mom. "We don't even know yet if we can afford one."

"But I can use it to earn money to help pay for it," suggested Michael. "Remember last spring I plant-sat for Mrs. Smith's forty-two African violets while she went away?"

"Who could forget?" remarked Mom. "The dining room was wall-to-wall plants."

"With a greenhouse," he continued, "I could take care of a lot more. Like a dog kennel, only for plants, when people go on vacation."

"Good idea," said Dad.

"And with Stanley and Fluffy getting sunshine all day, they won't eat so many socks. That'll save money."

"There's one big problem we have to solve first," Dad said. "We promised the botanical garden to sell them two plants."

"Let's get some from Dr. Sparks. She's got lots," said Norman.

Mom said, "Those aren't big enough. The botanical garden wanted ours because they're the biggest and best specimens."

"I know where we could get another one," said Michael. "Grandma. She said hers is almost five feet tall."

Mom went into the kitchen to call her mother. When she explained the situation, Grandma said she would be glad to sell her plant. She promised to find a trucking company right away that would deliver it to them.

Norman said, "I know where we can get another big one."

"Where?" asked Dad. "There aren't any more."

"There's one," said Norman. "Jason's."

"Oh, no!" said Mom. "There's another one?"

"The evil twin?" said Michael. "Jason's starving it to death."

"Not anymore," said Norman. "I went back there and fed it one day and talked to it. I didn't get near it, though. Its vines are mostly grown back already. But I made Jason feed it after that."

"How?" asked Michael.

"I told him I'd tell his mother if he didn't. So he had to buy the socks. Every couple days on the way home from school, I go over there to see if the plant's OK. I talk to it. It's grown a little. It doesn't seem so mean. The last time I was there, it didn't try to grab me."

Michael said, "Great! Before the truck comes, we can go over there and dig it up. Jason will be glad to get rid of it."

Mom turned to the plants. "So," she said, "now that you two are permanent members of the family, I expect you to behave. If you want fudge ripple socks every night, you've got to be good. Act up, and it'll be oatmeal socks for a week."

Fluffy patted her on the head with a vine, the way he did with Norman.

"See!" exclaimed Norman. "He loves you!"

Chapter 20

The plants did behave well most of the time. They were allowed to help around the house by dusting, but only when the boys stood by to catch anything they knocked over.

By the end of October, the weather was cold almost every day, so the plants couldn't stay out. For Halloween Dad and Mom let the boys put king-sized sheets over Stanley and Fluffy. Greeting trick-or-treaters who came to the door, they were a big hit.

But Mom refused to consider Pilgrim costumes for Thanksgiving. Norman was disappointed, but he perked up when Michael suggested a Christmas plan.

"Stanley and Fluffy can be our Christmas tree," he said.

"Very funny," said Mom.

"No, really," he said. "We'll stand them together in the living room and decorate them. It'll save money if we don't have to buy a tree. They can do it every year."

Dad remarked, "They'd be an awfully odd-looking Christmas tree."

Norman said, "We'll have to undecorate them every night. If they eat the lights and ornaments, they'll die."

Michael replied, "Not if we make the decorations out of socks and don't string any lights on them."

"There would be one advantage," said Mom. "We wouldn't have to be vacuuming up pine needles every day."

Dad said, "And we wouldn't have to stand around arguing at the Christmas tree lot about which one to buy. Let's give Stanley and Fluffy a try."

On Christmas Eve the boys rolled the plants into the living room and started putting on the decorations they had bought—a dozen pairs of Christmas socks in tiny sizes. The different designs were of Santas, pine trees, snowmen, holly, and reindeer wearing ice skates. They split up the pairs and hung twelve different ones on each plant. Stanley didn't like where Michael hung one sock. The plant plucked it off and handed it back to him. Michael tried a different spot. Stanley seemed to find that more comfortable.

"Maybe they won't eat these Christmas socks," said Michael. "They'll have their regular ones to eat."

"I hope so," said Norman. "That way we won't have to buy new decorations every day."

Mom and Dad agreed that the plants looked pretty good. All evening neighbors dropped in for eggnog and goodies. Some of them probably thought it was weird to use the plants as Christmas trees, and socks for decorations, but they were too polite to say so.

When the Kramers stopped in, Kyle did not lunge for the plants. He pointed up at the little red and green socks hanging on them and said, "Pitty, pitty!"

Michael took a pair down and gave them to him. His

mother took his shoes and socks off and put the new socks on. Kyle was so delighted that he ran around the living room beaming. He refused to let his mother put his shoes back on.

After everyone went home, Michael hung eight fudge ripple socks along the mantel over the fireplace.

Dad said, "We're not putting the presents under the plants tonight. We'll keep them in the dining room with the door closed and bring them out in the morning."

Norman said, "I just wrote a poem."

"You didn't write anything down," replied Michael.

"I wrote it in my mind," insisted Norman.

"OK," said Dad. "Let's hear it."

Norman stood in front of the fireplace, cleared his throat, and recited: "The stockings were hung by the chimney with care. But they would be gone when Santa got there."

They all burst out laughing. "That's a good one," said Dad. "You better write that down."

Soon Norman began pestering Mom and Dad to let him open one present.

To shut him up, Mom finally said, "All right. You can both open the gifts Grandma sent you."

Norman ran into the dining room. Sounds of ripping paper and cardboard were followed by a loud "Yippee!" Then from the dining room rolled a remote-controlled truck, trailed by Norman with the control.

"This is great!" he said. He sent it running around from room to room. It kept bumping into walls and furniture as he tried to get the control under control.

Michael brought his present into the living room and ripped it open.

"Oh, no," said Mom. "Another one."

131

Michael sent his truck off down the hall.

Dad sighed. He said to Mom, "You know what's coming."

"Yes," she said. "Truck races. Truck crashes. Dueling trucks. And nicks in the furniture."

They made the boys park their new toys in the dining room and go to bed.

Late that night, Mom, Dad, Michael, and Norman were nestled all snug in their beds. Perhaps even visions of sugarplums danced in their heads. But Stanley and Fluffy made such a clatter that Norman woke up to see what was the matter.

When he stepped into the hall, he almost got run over by a speeding plant. Stanley was hanging on to a truck with two vines and operating the control with two others. In the living room, Fluffy was hanging on to the other truck and running it around, bumping into furniture. Stanley zoomed back into the living room and knocked over a lamp. They were having a Christmas tree race.

Avon Camelot Presents
Award-Winning Author

THEODORE TAYLOR

THE CAY 00142-X/$3.99 US/$4.99 Can

After being blinded in a fatal shipwreck, Phillip was rescued from the shark-infested waters by the kindly old black man who had worked on deck. Cast up on a remote island, together they began an amazing adventure.

THE TROUBLE WITH TUCK
62711-6/$3.50 US/$4.25 Can

Twice Helen's dog Tuck had saved her life. And when she discovered he was going blind, she fought to become his eyes—now it was her turn to save *his* life.

TUCK TRIUMPHANT 71323-3/$3.50 US/$4.25 Can

At last...the miracle dog returns in the heartwarming sequel to *The Trouble with Tuck*.

Coming Soon

MARIA 72120-1/$3.50 US/$4.50 Can